PENGUIN CLASSICS

Maigret and the Good Peop

T0249284

'Extraordinary masterpieces of tl.
— John Banville

'A brilliant writer'
— India Knight

'Intense atmosphere and resonant detail . . . make Simenon's
fiction remarkably like life'
— Julian Barnes

'A truly wonderful writer . . . marvellously readable – lucid,
simple, absolutely in tune with the world he creates'
— Muriel Spark

'Few writers have ever conveyed with such a sure touch, the
bleakness of human life'
— A. N. Wilson

'Compelling, remorseless, brilliant'
— John Gray

'A writer of genius, one whose simplicity of language creates
indelible images that the florid stylists of our own day can
only dream of'
— *Daily Mail*

'The mysteries of the human personality are revealed in all
their disconcerting complexity'
— Anita Brookner

'One of the greatest writers of our time'
— *The Sunday Times*

'I love reading Simenon. He makes me think of Chekhov'
— William Faulkner

'One of the great psychological novelists of this century'
— *Independent*

'The greatest of all, the most genuine novelist we have had
in literature'
— André Gide

'Simenon ought to be spoken of in the same breath as
Camus, Beckett and Kafka'
— *Independent on Sunday*

GEORGES SIMENON

Maigret and the Good People of Montparnasse

Translated by ROS SCHWARTZ

PENGUIN BOOKS

PENGUIN CLASSICS

UK | USA | Canada | Ireland | Australia
India | New Zealand | South Africa

Penguin Books is part of the Penguin Random House group of companies
whose addresses can be found at global.penguinrandomhouse.com.

Penguin
Random House
UK

First published in French as *Maigret et les braves gens* by Presses de la Cité 1962
This translation first published 2018

004

Copyright © Georges Simenon Limited, 1962
Translation copyright © Ros Schwartz, 2018
GEORGES SIMENON ® Simenon.tm
MAIGRET ® Georges Simenon Limited
All rights reserved

The moral rights of the author and translator have been asserted

Set in 12.5/15 pt Dante MT Std
Typeset by Jouve (UK), Milton Keynes
Printed and bound in Great Britain by Clays Ltd, Elcograf S.p.A.

ISBN: 978-0-241-30393-1

Maigret and the Good People of Montparnasse

1.

Instead of groaning and fumbling for the telephone in the dark as he usually did when it rang in the middle of the night, Maigret gave a sigh of relief.

Already he could only vaguely recall the dream from which he'd been so rudely awakened, but he knew it had been unpleasant: he'd been trying to explain to someone important, whose face he couldn't see and who was extremely displeased with him, that it wasn't his fault, that he needed to be shown patience, just a few days' patience, because he was out of practice and he felt listless, ill at ease with himself. He needed to be trusted and it wouldn't be long. Most of all, he needed not to be looked at in a disapproving or mocking way . . .

'Hello . . .'

As he pressed the receiver to his ear, Madame Maigret raised herself up on her elbow and switched on the bedside light.

'Maigret?' inquired a voice.

'Yes.'

He didn't recognize the caller, even though it sounded familiar.

'Saint-Hubert here . . .'

A detective inspector of around his age, whom he'd known since his early days. They addressed one another by their surnames and remained quite formal. Saint-Hubert was tall and thin, auburn-haired and a little slow and solemn, keen to dot the i's and cross the t's.

'Have I woken you?'

'Yes.'

'My apologies. In any case, I think that Quai des Orfèvres will be in touch any minute to fill you in because I've alerted the public prosecutor's office and the Police Judiciaire.'

Sitting up now, Maigret reached for a pipe that he'd left on the bedside table to burn itself out when he'd gone to bed. He looked around for matches. Madame Maigret rose and went to fetch some from the mantelpiece. The air blowing in through the open window was still balmy; the city was studded with lights and the rumble of distant taxis could be heard.

They had come home from their holiday five days earlier and this was the first time they'd been woken up so abruptly. For Maigret, it was a sort of coming back down to earth, a return to routine.

'What's happened?' he muttered, drawing on his pipe while his wife held the lit match over the bowl.

'I'm phoning from the apartment of Monsieur René Josselin, 37a, Rue Notre-Dame-des-Champs, next door to the convent of the Little Sisters of the Poor . . . A body has just been discovered. I don't know much about it because I only got here twenty minutes ago . . . Can you hear me?'

'Yes . . .'

Madame Maigret went into the kitchen to make coffee and Maigret gave her a knowing wink.

'The case looks disturbing; it is probably sensitive . . . That's why I took the liberty of calling you . . . I was afraid they'd simply send one of the duty inspectors . . .'

He chose his words carefully and Maigret guessed that he wasn't alone in the room.

'I knew you were on holiday recently.'

'I returned last week.'

It was Wednesday. Or rather Thursday, because the alarm clock on Madame Maigret's bedside table showed ten past two. They had gone to the cinema, not so much to see the film, which was mediocre, but to get back into the habit of going out.

'Do you intend to come?'

'As soon as I'm dressed.'

'I will be most grateful to you. I know the Josselins slightly. They're not the sort of people one expects to be involved in a tragedy like this . . .'

Even the smell of the tobacco had a professional quality to it: that of a pipe put out the previous evening and re-lit in the middle of the night when a man is woken up by an emergency. The aroma of coffee too was different from that of the morning coffee. And the smell of petrol, wafting in through the open window . . .

For the past eight days, Maigret had felt as if he were floundering. This time, they had spent three entire weeks at Meung-sur-Loire without once hearing from the Police Judiciaire, without Maigret being summoned back to Paris on an urgent case, as had happened in previous years.

They'd carried on doing up the house and working on

5

the garden. Maigret had gone fishing and played belote with the locals and now he was finding it hard to get back to normal.

So was Paris, it seemed. It was not raining; nor was there the usual post-holiday coolness. The big tourist buses continued to ferry foreigners in loud shirts through the streets and, although a lot of Parisians were back, others were still leaving the city by the trainload.

The Police Judiciaire and the office appeared a little unreal, and Maigret sometimes wondered what he was doing there, as if real life was back on the banks of the Loire.

It was probably this unease that was the cause of his dream, the details of which he was trying in vain to recollect. Madame Maigret came back from the kitchen with a cup of scalding coffee and immediately grasped that, far from being furious at being woken up so brutally, he was pleased.

'Where is it?'

'In Montparnasse . . . Rue Notre-Dame-des-Champs.'

He had put on his shirt and trousers and was lacing up his shoes when the telephone rang again. This time, it was the Police Judiciaire.

'Torrence here, chief . . . We've just been informed that—'

'That a man has been killed in Rue Notre-Dame-des-Champs.'

'You know? Are you going over there?'

'Who's in the office?'

'There's Dupeu, who's in the middle of questioning a

suspect in the jewellery heist case, then Vacher . . . Hold on . . . Lapointe's just come in—'

'Tell him to go there and wait for me.'

Janvier was on holiday. Lucas, back the previous day, hadn't yet returned to work.

'Shall I phone for a taxi?' asked Madame Maigret a little later.

In the street, he found a driver who knew him, and for once he was pleased.

'Where to, inspector?'

He gave the address and filled a fresh pipe. On arrival in Rue Notre-Dame-des-Champs, he spotted a little Police Judiciaire car and Lapointe standing on the pavement, smoking a cigarette and chatting with a police officer.

'Third floor on the left,' said the policeman.

Maigret and Lapointe entered the well-maintained middle-class apartment building. There was a light in the lodge, and through the net curtain Maigret thought he recognized an inspector from the 6th arrondissement questioning the concierge.

As soon as the lift stopped, a door opened and Saint-Hubert stepped forward to greet them.

'The public prosecutor won't be here for another half an hour . . . Come in . . . You will understand why I insisted on telephoning you . . .'

They entered a spacious hallway, then Saint-Hubert pushed a half-open door and they found themselves in a peaceful drawing room where there was no one except for the body of a man slumped in a leather armchair. Tall-ish, quite portly, he was hunched up, his head lolling to one side and his eyes open.

7

'I asked the family to withdraw to another room . . . Madame Josselin is being attended to by the family physician, Doctor Larue, who happens to be a friend of mine.'

'Was she injured?'

'No. She wasn't here when the tragedy occurred. I'll quickly put you in the picture.'

'Who lives in the apartment? How many people?'

'Two.'

'You mentioned the family . . .'

'You'll see . . . Monsieur and Madame Josselin have lived here on their own since their daughter got married. She married a young doctor, a paediatrician, Doctor Fabre, who is assistant to Professor Baron at the Hospital for Sick Children.'

Lapointe took notes.

'This evening, Madame Josselin and her daughter went to the Théâtre de la Madeleine—'

'What about the husbands?'

'René Josselin stayed on his own for a while.'

'Didn't he like the theatre?'

'I don't know. I think rather that he didn't like going out in the evening.'

'What was his occupation?'

'For the past two years, he had none. He used to own a cardboard factory, in Rue du Saint-Gothard. He made cardboard boxes, especially luxury packaging for perfumers, for example. He sold his business, for health reasons . . .'

'How old?'

Sixty-five or sixty-six . . . So last night, he stayed in on his own . . . Then his son-in-law joined him, I don't know at what time, and the two men played chess.'

There was a chess board on a little table with the pieces positioned as if a game had been interrupted.

Saint-Hubert spoke quietly, and people could be heard coming and going in other rooms whose doors were not fully closed.

'When the two women came back from the theatre—'

'At what time?'

'A quarter past midnight . . . As I was saying, when they came back, they found René Josselin just as you see him in here—'

'How many bullets?'

'Two . . . Both close to the heart.'

'Didn't the other residents hear anything?'

'The next-door neighbours are still on holiday.'

'Were you called straight away?'

'No. First of all they telephoned Doctor Larue. He lives around the corner in Rue d'Assas and Josselin was in his care. That took a while and it was only at ten past one that I received a call from my station, which had just been informed. I quickly got dressed and made my way here . . . I only asked a few questions because it was difficult, given the state Madame Josselin is in—'

'The son-in-law?'

'He arrived shortly before you did.'

'What does he say?'

'It was hard to reach him, but he was eventually found at the hospital where he had gone to see a sick child, a case of encephalitis, I believe—'

'Where is he now?'

'In there.'

Saint-Hubert pointed to one of the doors. They could hear whispering.

'From the little I gleaned, nothing has been stolen and we found no signs of a break-in. The Josselins are not aware of having any enemies . . . They are good people, who live an uneventful life.'

There was a knock at the door. It was Ledent, a young forensic pathologist whom Maigret knew. He shook hands all round then set his bag down on a chest of drawers and opened it.

'I received a phone call from the prosecutor's office,' he said. 'The deputy public prosecutor's on his way.'

'I'd like to ask the young lady some questions,' muttered Maigret whose eyes had swept the room several times.

He understood Saint-Hubert's feelings. The setting was not only elegant and comfortable, it exuded peace and quiet and family life. It was not a formal drawing room; it was a room that was pleasant to be in and where each piece of furniture had a purpose and a history.

The huge tan leather armchair, for example, was obviously the one that René Josselin was in the habit of sitting in every evening, and, facing it, on the other side of the room, the television set was just within his field of vision.

The grand piano had been played for years by a little girl whose portrait was on the wall and, next to another armchair not as deep as that of the paterfamilias, was a pretty, finely wrought Louis XV table.

'Do you want me to call her in?'

'I'd rather talk to her in another room.'

Saint-Hubert knocked on a door, vanished for a moment, and came back to fetch Maigret, who caught a glimpse of a bedroom, and a man leaning over a woman lying on the bed.

Another woman, younger, came over to Maigret and murmured:

'If you'd like to follow me into my former bedroom . . .'

A bedroom that was still that of a little girl, full of mementos, knick-knacks and photographs, as if her parents had wanted her, once married, to be able to come back and find her childhood room.

'You are Detective Chief Inspector Maigret, aren't you?'

He nodded.

'You may smoke your pipe . . . My husband smokes cigarettes all day long, except at the bedsides of his young patients, of course.'

She was wearing an elegant dress and had had her hair done before going to the theatre. Her hands plucked at a handkerchief.

'Would you rather remain standing?'

'Yes . . . You would too, wouldn't you?'

Unable to keep still, she paced up and down, not knowing where to rest her gaze.

'I don't know whether you can imagine the effect on us . . . You hear about murders every day through the papers, the wireless, but you don't imagine for one minute that it can happen to you . . . Poor Papa!'

'Were you very close to your father?'

'He was an exceptionally generous man . . . I meant the

world to him . . . I am his only child . . . You must find out what happened, Monsieur Maigret, and tell us . . . I can't get out of my head that it is all a terrible mistake.'

'Do you think the murderer could have come to the wrong floor?'

She looked at him like someone grasping a lifeline but immediately shook her head.

'It's not possible . . . The lock wasn't forced . . . My father must have opened the door . . .'

Maigret called out:

'Lapointe! . . . You can come in.'

He introduced him and Lapointe blushed at finding himself in a girl's room.

'May I ask you a few questions? Whose idea was it to go to the theatre, yours or your mother's?'

'It's hard to say. I think it was mother's. She's always the one who insists that I should go out. I have two children, the eldest is three, the baby ten months. When my husband isn't at his surgery, where I don't see him, he's out and about, at the hospital or visiting his patients. He's a man who devotes himself entirely to his work. So, occasionally, two or three times a month, mother telephones to invite me to go out with her.'

'This evening there was a play I wanted to see at—'

'Was your husband not free?'

'Not before nine thirty. That was too late. Besides, he doesn't like the theatre.'

'What time did you come here?'

'At around eight thirty.'

'Where do you live?'

'Boulevard Brune, near the Cité Universitaire.'

'Did you take a taxi?'

'No. My husband drove me here in his car. He had a gap between appointments.'

'Did he come up?'

'He dropped me off outside.'

'Was he planning to pick you up afterwards?'

'It was almost always the same when my mother and I went out. Paul – that's my husband – would join my father as soon as he finished his visits and the pair of them played chess or watched television until our return.'

'Is that what happened last night?'

'From what he has just told me, yes. He arrived just after nine thirty. They started a game. Then my husband received a telephone call—'

'At what time?'

'He hasn't had the chance to tell me. He left, and when mother and I came upstairs later, we were met with the scene that you saw . . .'

'Where was your husband at that time?'

'I telephoned home immediately and Germaine, our maid, told me he wasn't back yet.'

'Did it not occur to you to inform the police?'

'I don't know . . . Mother and I didn't know what to do . . . We didn't understand . . . We needed someone to advise us and it was my idea to call Doctor Larue . . . He's both a friend and Papa's physician.'

'Weren't you surprised by your husband's absence?'

'At first I told myself he must have been called out to an emergency . . . Then, when Doctor Larue was here, I telephoned the hospital . . . That's where I managed to get hold of him.'

'How did he react?'

'He said he'd come straight away . . . Doctor Larue had already called the police . . . I'm not sure I'm telling you all this in the right order . . . At the same time, I was looking after mother, who seemed not to know where she was.'

'How old is she?'

'Fifty-one. She's a lot younger than father, who married late, at thirty-five—'

'Would you send your husband in to see me?'

Through the open door, Maigret could hear voices in the drawing room, those of the deputy public prosecutor, Mercier, and Étienne Gossard, a young examining magistrate who, like the others, had been dragged from his bed. The forensics team from Criminal Records would soon be taking over the room.

'Did you want to see me?'

The man was young, thin and anxious. His wife had come back in with him and asked timidly:

'May I stay?'

Maigret nodded.

'I'm told, doctor, that you arrived here at around nine thirty.'

'A little later, not much.'

'Had you finished for the day?'

'I thought I had, but in my profession you can never be certain.'

'I presume that when you leave your apartment, you give your maid an address where you can be contacted?'

'Germaine knew I was here.'

'Is she your maid?'

'Yes. She also looks after the children when my wife isn't there.'

'How did your father-in-law seem?'

'The same as usual. He was watching television. The programme was of no interest and he suggested a game of chess. We started playing. At around ten fifteen, the telephone rang.'

'Was it for you?'

'Yes. Germaine told me that I was needed urgently at 28, Rue Julie . . . That's in my neighbourhood . . . Germaine hadn't caught the name, Lesage or Lechat, or perhaps Lachat . . . The person who called sounded distraught.'

'Did you leave immediately?'

'Yes. I told my father-in-law that I'd be back if my patient didn't take up too much time, otherwise I'd go straight home . . . That was my intention . . . I get up very early, because of the hospital.'

'How long did you stay with your patient?'

'There was no patient. I asked a concierge, who looked at me in surprise and said that no one with the name Lesage or Lachat lived there, and that she was not aware of any sick child.'

'What did you do?'

'I asked permission to telephone home and I questioned Germaine again . . . She repeated that it was definitely number 28 . . . Just in case, I rang at 18 and 38, with no success . . . Since I was out anyway, I decided to drop in at the hospital to see a young patient I was concerned about—'

'What time was that?'

'I don't know . . . I spent about half an hour at the child's bedside and after that went on a ward round with one of the nurses . . . Then I was told that my wife was on the phone . . .'

'You are the last person to have seen your father-in-law alive . . . Did he seem worried at all?'

'Not in the least . . . On showing me out, he told me he was going to finish the game on his own . . . I heard him putting the chain on the door.'

'Are you certain?'

'I heard the rattle of the chain . . . I'd swear I did.'

'So he must have got up to open the door to his murderer . . . Tell me, madame, when you arrived with your mother, I presume the chain was not on?'

'How would we have got in?'

The doctor was puffing rapidly on his cigarette, lighting another one before he had stubbed out the first, staring worriedly at the rug and then at Maigret. He looked like a man desperately grappling with a problem, and his wife was just as agitated as he was.

'Tomorrow I'll have to go over these questions in detail, I'm sorry,' said Maigret.

'I understand.'

'Now I must get back to the gentlemen from the prosecutor's office.'

'Are they going to remove the body?'

'They have to . . .'

No one used the word autopsy, but it was clear that the young woman was thinking it.

'Go back to Madame Josselin. I'll speak to her briefly later and I'll be as quick as I can.'

In the drawing room, Maigret automatically shook hands and greeted his colleagues from Criminal Records, who were setting up their equipment.

Troubled, the examining magistrate asked:

'What do you think, Maigret?'

'Nothing.'

'Don't you find it strange that the son-in-law should be called out to a non-existent patient that evening? How well did he get on with his father-in-law?'

'I don't know.'

He hated being asked these questions when they had all just intruded on a family's privacy.

The inspector he had glimpsed in the concierge's lodge came into the room, notebook in hand, and walked over to Maigret and Saint-Hubert.

'The concierge is positive,' he said. 'I've been question-ing her for nearly an hour. She's a bright young woman whose husband is a police officer. He's on duty tonight.'

'What does she say?'

'She opened the door to Doctor Fabre at nine thirty-five. She's certain of the time because she was about to go to bed and was winding up the alarm-clock. She tends to retire early because her baby, who's only three months old, wakes her very early in the morning for his first feed.

'She was asleep at ten fifteen, when the bell rang. Doctor Fabre said his name as he went past and she recognized his voice.'

'How many people came in and went out afterwards?'

'Wait. She tried to go back to sleep. She was just dozing off when the bell rang again, from the street this time. The person who came in said their name: Aresco. That's a South American family who live on the first floor. Almost immediately afterwards, the baby woke up. She couldn't get him back to sleep so she heated up some sugar water. No one came in and no one went out until Madame Josselin and her daughter returned.'

The magistrates, who had been listening, exchanged grave looks.

'In other words,' said the examining magistrate, 'Doctor Fabre is the last person to have left the building?'

'Madame Bonnet – that's the name of the concierge – is certain. Had she slept, she wouldn't have been so categorical. But because of the baby, she was up the entire time.'

'Was she still up when the two ladies returned? Did the child stay awake for two hours?'

'Apparently. She was even worried about him and wished she'd seen Doctor Fabre so she could have asked his advice.'

They looked questioningly at Maigret, who had an irritable expression.

'Have you found the cartridges?' he asked, turning to one of the forensics experts.

'Two cartridges . . . 6.35 . . . Can we remove the body?'

The men in white coats were waiting with their

stretcher. As René Josselin was taken out of his front door under a sheet, his daughter entered the room noiselessly. Her gaze met that of Maigret, who went over to her.

'Why are you here?'

She didn't answer right away. She watched the stretcher bearers. Only once the door had closed behind them did she whisper, a little like someone speaking in a dream:

'An idea occurred to me . . . Wait . . .'

She went over to an antique chest of drawers between two windows and opened the top drawer.

'What are you looking for?'

Her lips trembled, and she looked intently at Maigret.

'The revolver . . .'

'Was there a revolver in that drawer?'

'For years . . . That's why, when I was little, the drawer was always locked.'

'What kind of revolver?'

'A very flat automatic, blue-coloured, a Belgian make.'

'A Browning 6.35?'

'I think so . . . I'm not sure . . . It was engraved with the word Herstal and some numbers.'

The men exchanged more looks, because the description was that of a 6.35 automatic.

'When was the last time you saw it?'

'A while ago . . . Weeks . . . Maybe even months . . . Probably one evening when we were playing cards, because the cards were in the same drawer . . . They're still there . . . Here, things stay in the same place for a long time.'

'But the automatic isn't there now?'

'No.'

'So the person who used it knew where to find it?'

'Perhaps it was my father who took it to defend himself.'

They could read the fear in her eyes.

'Your parents don't have any servants?'

'They used to have a maid, who got married around six months ago. Since then, they've tried two others. Mother wasn't satisfied and decided to hire a cleaner instead, Madame Manu. She comes at seven in the morning and leaves at eight o'clock at night.'

All this was normal, natural, except that this quiet man, who had recently retired, had been murdered in his armchair.

There was something that didn't quite add up about the tragedy, something incongruous.

'How is your mother?'

'Doctor Larue made her go to bed. She won't say a word and stares fixedly, as if she had lost consciousness. She hasn't cried. She seems vacant . . . The doctor requests your permission to give her a sedative . . . He'd rather she slept . . . May he?'

Why not? It wasn't by asking Madame Josselin a few questions that Maigret would find out the truth.

'He may,' he replied.

The forensics team worked with their usual quiet meticulousness. The deputy public prosecutor took his leave.

'Are you coming, Gossard? Have you got your car?'

'No. I came by taxi.'

'I'll drive you back, if you like.'

Saint-Hubert left too, muttering to Maigret on his way out:

'Was I right to call you?'

Maigret nodded and went and sat down in an armchair.

'Open the window,' he said to Lapointe.

It was warm in the room and suddenly he was surprised that despite the summery temperature, Josselin had spent the evening with all the windows shut.

'Call the son-in-law.'

'Right away, chief.'

Fabre soon arrived, looking exhausted.

'Tell me, doctor, when you left your father-in-law, were the windows open or closed?'

He thought, and looked at the two windows, whose curtains were drawn.

'Wait . . . I don't know . . . I'm trying to remember . . . I was sitting here . . . I believe I could see lights . . . Yes . . . I could almost swear that the left-hand window was open . . . I could distinctly hear the sounds of the city.'

'And you didn't close it before leaving?'

'Why would I have done that?'

'I don't know.'

'No . . . It didn't occur to me . . . You forget that this is not my home.'

'Did you often come here?'

'About once a week . . . Véronique visited her father and her mother more frequently . . . Tell me . . . My wife is going to sleep here tonight, but I would rather sleep at home . . . We never leave the children alone with the maid at night . . . Besides, I have to be at the hospital at seven tomorrow morning.'

'What's stopping you from leaving?'

He was surprised by this question, as if he considered himself a suspect.

'Thank you.'

He could be heard talking to his wife in the next room, then he walked across the drawing room, bareheaded, holding his bag, and said goodbye with an embarrassed air.

2.

Once the three men had left the building, only Madame Josselin and her daughter remained in the apartment. After a restless night the concierge's baby must have fallen asleep because the lodge was in darkness, and Maigret's finger hovered over the bell.

'How about going for a drink, doctor?'

Lapointe, about to open the door of the black car, froze before gripping the handle. Doctor Larue looked at his watch, as if it would decide for him.

'I'd be delighted to have a cup of coffee,' he said in the deep, mellifluous voice that he used with his patients. 'There must be a bar that's still open on the corner of Boulevard Montparnasse.'

It was not yet daybreak. The streets were almost empty. Maigret glanced up at the third floor and saw the lights go off in the drawing room, where one of the windows was still open.

Would Véronique Fabre get undressed and go to bed in her old room? Or would she stay at the bedside of her mother, who had been knocked out by the doctor's jab? What were her thoughts in the now empty rooms where so many strangers had been going about their work earlier?

'Bring the car,' Maigret said to Lapointe.

They only had to go down Rue Vavin. Larue and Maigret walked along the street. The doctor was a shortish, plump man with broad shoulders who probably never lost his air of calm, his dignity or his mild manner. Maigret could tell he was used to a well-heeled clientele, whose manner and ways he had adopted, not without exaggerating them somewhat.

Although he was around fifty, there was still a great deal of innocence in his blue eyes, a certain fear too of upsetting people, and later Maigret would learn that each year he exhibited at the Doctor-Painters' art show.

'Have you known the Josselins long?'

'Since I moved to this neighbourhood, which was around twenty years ago. Véronique was still a little girl and, if my memory serves me correctly, the first time they called me out was for her, when she had measles.'

It was the chill, slightly damp hour. The gas lamps were haloed with a soft glow. Several cars were parked on the corner of Boulevard Raspail outside a cabaret which was still open; the liveried doorman standing at the entrance took the two men for potential clients. He opened the door, letting out gusts of music.

Lapointe kept abreast of them in the little car, and drew up alongside the kerb.

The Montparnasse night was not entirely over. A couple were arguing in hushed tones against a wall, close to a hotel. In the still-lit bar, as the doctor had anticipated, a few shapes could be seen and an elderly flower-seller at the bar was drinking a coffee and rum that gave off a strong smell of alcohol.

'A brandy and water for me,' said Maigret.

The doctor hesitated.

'I think I'll have the same, dammit!'

'What about you, Lapointe?'

'Same for me, chief.'

'Three brandies and water.'

They sat down at a pedestal table near the window and began talking quietly while the nocturnal wheeling and dealing carried on around them. Larue stated with conviction:

'They're good people. We quickly became friends, and my wife and I are often invited there for dinner.'

'Are they wealthy?'

'It all depends what you mean by wealthy. They are certainly very well-off. René Josselin's father already owned a little packaging business in Rue du Saint-Gothard, a simple glazed workshop at the far end of a courtyard, which employed around ten women. When he inherited it, René bought modern equipment. He was a man of taste, who was not lacking in ideas, and he soon built up a clientele of famous perfumers and other luxury goods houses.'

'I understand he married late, at around thirty-five?'

'That's correct. He carried on living above the workshops in Rue du Saint-Gothard with his mother, who had always been an invalid. He did not conceal from me that she was the reason he hadn't married sooner. On the one hand, he didn't want to leave her on her own, and on the other, he didn't feel he had the right to impose his sick mother on a young wife. He worked very hard, and lived solely for his business.'

'To your health.'

'To yours.'

Lapointe, his eyes a little bloodshot from tiredness, didn't miss a word of the conversation.

'He got married after his mother died, and moved to Rue Notre-Dame-des-Champs.'

'Who was his wife?'

'Francine de Lancieux, the daughter of a former colonel. I think they lived close by, in Rue du Saint-Gothard or Rue Dareau, and that was how Josselin met her. She must have been twenty-two at the time.'

'Did they get along well?'

'They were one of the closest couples I have ever known. Almost immediately, they had a daughter, Véronique, whom you met this evening. Later, they hoped to have a son, but a rather serious operation put an end to their hopes.'

Good people, Saint-Hubert had said, and now the doctor. People who lived a quiet, uneventful life, in calm, well-to-do surroundings.

'They came back from La Baule last week . . . They bought a house there when Véronique was still a little girl, and they continued to go there every year. Now that Véronique has become a mother too, they take her children there.'

'What about the husband?'

'Doctor Fabre? I don't know whether he took a holiday, probably no longer than a week if he did. Perhaps he joined them a couple of times from Saturday to Sunday evening. He's a man who is entirely dedicated to medicine

26

and to his patients, a sort of secular saint. When he met Véronique, he was a junior doctor at the Hospital for Sick Children and, if he weren't married, he would probably have been content with a hospital career, without taking on private patients.'

'Do you think his wife insisted he have a private practice?'

'I won't be breaking patient confidentiality in answering that question. Fabre makes no secret of it. If he'd devoted himself solely to the hospital, he would have struggled to support a family. His father-in-law wanted him to take over a practice and lent him the money. You have seen him. He isn't bothered about his appearance, or about comfort. He generally wears crumpled clothes and, left to his own devices, I suspect he'd forget to change his underwear . . .'

'Did he get along well with Josselin?'

'The two men respected each other. Josselin was proud of his son-in-law and, on top of that, they were both keen chess players.'

'Was he seriously ill?'

'I was the one who asked him to cut down on his activity. He has always been fat and I have known him to weigh over one hundred and ten kilos. That didn't stop him working twelve or thirteen hours a day. His heart couldn't cope. Two years ago, he had a heart attack, which was fairly minor, but still it was a warning.

'I advised him to take on a business partner and to confine himself to a supervisory role, just to keep his mind occupied.

'To my great surprise, he chose to give up altogether. He said he was incapable of doing things by halves.'

'Did he sell his business?'

'To two of his employees. Since they didn't have enough money, he retained a stake for a certain number of years, I don't know how long exactly.'

'How did he spend his time over the past two years?'

'In the morning, he'd go for a stroll in the Luxembourg Gardens; I often used to see him there. He walked slowly, cautiously, as many people with heart disease do, because he ended up exaggerating his condition. He read. You saw his bookshelves. He'd never had the time to read before, and now he was discovering literature belatedly and talked about it enthusiastically.'

'His wife?'

'Even though they had a maid and then a cleaning woman after they decided to do without a live-in servant, she kept very busy with the home and the cooking. And she would go almost every day to Boulevard Brune to see her grandchildren. She'd take the eldest one in her car to the Parc Montsouris . . .'

'You must have been surprised when you heard what had happened?'

'I still can't believe it. I have witnessed tragedies among my patients, not often, but still there have been a few. But they were never entirely unexpected, if you see what I mean. In each case, appearances belied some kind of fragility, some kind of disturbance. This time, I don't know what to think.'

Maigret signalled to the waiter to refill their glasses.

'Madame Josselin's reaction worries me,' went on the doctor, still with the same smoothness. 'Or rather I'd say her lack of reaction, her listlessness. I haven't been able to get a word out of her all evening. She watched us, her daughter, her son-in-law and me, as if she couldn't see us. She didn't shed a tear. From her room, we could hear the noises from the drawing room. It wasn't difficult, with a bit of imagination, to guess what was happening in there, the photographers' flash bulbs popping, for example, then, when they removed the body . . .

'I thought that at that point at least she would react, try to rush out. She was conscious and yet she didn't budge, didn't make the slightest movement . . .

'She has spent most of her life with a man and then, on returning from the theatre, she finds herself alone all of a sudden . . .

'I wonder how she's going to manage . . .'

'Do you think her daughter will take her to live with her?'

'It's not really possible. The Fabres live in one of those new buildings where the apartments are quite small. Naturally she loves her daughter and she's crazy about her grandchildren, but I can't see her living with them all the time . . . I really must go home now . . . Later this morning my patients will be waiting for me . . . No! Leave that . . .'

He had taken his wallet out of his pocket, but Maigret had been faster.

People were coming out of the cabaret next door, a whole crowd – musicians, dancers – waiting for one another or saying goodnight, and the pavement echoed with the clicking of very high heels.

Lapointe slid behind the wheel next to a Maigret whose expression was blank.

'To your place?'

'Yes.'

They were silent for a long time as the car drove through the empty streets.

'Tomorrow morning, early, I'd like someone to go to Rue Notre-Dame-des-Champs and question the residents as they get up. It is possible that someone heard the shots but wasn't worried because they thought it was a car backfiring . . . I'd also like to know the residents' movements from nine thirty p.m. onwards.'

'I'll take care of it myself, chief.'

'No. You must go to bed after passing on my instructions. If Torrence is free, send him to Rue Julie, to the three apartments whose doorbells Doctor Fabre says he rang.'

'Understood.'

'For the sake of thoroughness, it would be best to check what time he arrived at the hospital.'

'Is that all?'

'Yes . . . Yes and no . . . I have the feeling I've forgotten something but, for the past fifteen minutes at least, I've been asking myself what . . . It's an impression I've had several times during the course of the evening . . . At one point, I had an idea, or the beginning of an idea, and then someone spoke to me, Saint-Hubert if I'm not mistaken . . . By the time I'd answered him, I couldn't for the life of me pick up my train of thought.'

They reached Boulevard Richard-Lenoir. The window was still open on to the darkness of the bedroom, just as the window of the Josselin's drawing room had remained open after the departure of the deputy public prosecutor.

'Good night, Lapointe.'

'Good night, chief.'

'I probably won't be in the office before ten tomorrow.'

He climbed the stairs with heavy steps, vague thoughts going around and around in his mind, and he found the door open and Madame Maigret standing there in her nightdress.

'Not too tired?' she asked.

'I don't think so . . . No . . .'

It wasn't tiredness. He was preoccupied, uneasy, a little sad, as if the tragedy of Rue Notre-Dame-des-Champs affected him personally. The chubby-cheeked doctor had put it in a nutshell: the Josselins were not the sort of people you would expect to be caught up in a tragedy of this kind.

He mulled over the reactions of the various family members, that of Véronique, her husband, and Madame Josselin, whom he hadn't yet seen and had not even asked to see.

There was something awkward about all this. He felt awkward, for instance, about verifying Doctor Fabre's statement, as if he were a suspect.

And yet, going by the facts, suspicion fell on him. The deputy public prosecutor and examining magistrate Gossard had certainly thought so and, if they had said nothing, it was because this case made them feel as uncomfortable as it did Maigret.

Who knew that the two women, the mother and the daughter, were at the theatre that evening? Few people, probably, and so far, no names had been mentioned.

Fabre had arrived at Rue Notre-Dame-des-Champs at around nine thirty in the evening. He had begun a game of chess with his father-in-law.

He had received a phone call from his home to tell him that he had a patient to see in Rue Julie. There was nothing unusual in that. Like all doctors, he was probably often called away urgently.

But was it not a disturbing coincidence that the maid had misheard the name on that particular evening? And that she had sent the doctor to an address where no one needed him?'

Instead of returning to Rue Notre-Dame-des-Champs to finish the game and wait for his wife, Fabre had gone to the hospital. That too must happen often, given his nature.

During that time, only one resident came back into the building and said their name as they walked past the lodge. The concierge got up a little later and stated that no one had come in or gone out since.

'Aren't you asleep?'

'Not yet . . .'

'Are you sure you want to get up at nine?'

'Yes.'

It took him a long time to drop off. He kept picturing the thin silhouette of the paediatrician with crumpled clothes and the too-bright eyes of a man who doesn't get enough sleep.

Did he know he was the main suspect? And had it occurred to his wife and his mother-in-law?

Instead of telephoning the police on discovering the body, they had first of all called the apartment on Boulevard Brune. But they weren't aware of what had happened in Rue Julie. They didn't know why Fabre had left Rue Notre-Dame-des-Champs.

They hadn't immediately thought that he might be at the hospital and they had turned to the family physician, Doctor Larue.

What had they said to each other while they were alone with the body in the apartment? Was Madame Josselin already in a dazed state? Was it Véronique who had made the decisions on her own while her mother remained silent, staring vacantly into space?

Larue had arrived and immediately realized their error, if not negligence, in not calling the police. He was the one who had alerted the police station.

Maigret wished he could have seen and experienced this for himself. He had to reconstruct that night moment by moment.

Who had thought of calling the hospital and who had picked up the telephone? Larue? Véronique?

Who had checked to see if any valuables were missing from the apartment and whether a robbery had taken place?

Madame Josselin was taken into her bedroom. Larue stayed with her and eventually, with Maigret's permission, injected her with a sedative.

Fabre rushed over and found the police at his father-in-law's and the latter dead in his armchair.

'*And yet*,' thought Maigret as he dozed off, '*it was his wife who mentioned the automatic.*'

If Véronique hadn't opened the drawer deliberately, knowing what she was looking for, probably no one would have suspected the existence of the gun.

Now did that not rule out the possibility of a crime committed by a stranger?

Fabre claimed to have heard his father-in-law put the chain on the door after seeing him out, at 10.15.

So Josselin had opened the door to his murderer in person. He would not have been suspicious, because he went and sat back down in his armchair.

If the window was open at that point, as seemed likely, someone had closed it, either Josselin or his visitor.

And if the Browning was indeed the murder weapon, the killer knew it was kept in that precise place and would have been able to grab it without arousing suspicion.

Supposing a man had come in from outside, how did he leave the building?

Maigret finally fell into a restless sleep, tossing and turning heavily, and it was a relief to smell the aroma of coffee, to hear Madame Maigret's voice and see in front of him sunlit rooftops through the open window.

'It's nine o'clock . . .'

Within a second, he had called to mind every detail of the case, as if there had been no interruption.

'Pass me the telephone directory.'

He looked up the Josselins' number, dialled it and heard

the phone ring for quite a while before it was answered by a voice he didn't recognize.

'Is this Monsieur René Josselin's number?'

'He's dead.'

'Who's speaking?'

'Madame Manu, the cleaner.'

'Is Madame Fabre still there?'

'Who's asking for her?'

'Detective Chief Inspector Maigret, of the Police Judiciaire. I was there last night . . .'

'The young mistress has just left to go and change her clothes.'

'What about Madame Josselin?'

'She's still asleep. They've given her a drug and she's not supposed to wake up before her daughter gets back.'

'Have you had any visitors?'

'No one. I'm busy tidying up. I had no idea, when I got here this morning—'

'Thank you.'

Madame Maigret didn't ask him any questions and he merely said:

'A good man who's been murdered, God knows why . . .'

He recalled Josselin in his armchair. He tried to see him not dead but alive. Did he really sit there alone in front of the chess board, and did he carry on playing for a while, sometimes moving the black pieces and sometimes the white?

If he was waiting for someone . . . Knowing that his son-in-law would be coming to spend the evening with him, he couldn't have made a secret appointment. Unless . . .

Then it would appear that the telephone call asking Doctor Fabre to go to Rue Julie . . .

'It's the good people who give us the most trouble,' he grumbled as he finished his breakfast and made his way to the bathroom.

He didn't go straight to Quai des Orfèvres but simply telephoned to check he wasn't needed.

'Rue du Saint-Gothard,' he instructed the taxi-driver.

He was concentrating on René Josselin to begin with. True, Josselin was the victim, but a man isn't killed without reason.

Paris still had a holiday atmosphere. It was no longer the deserted Paris of August, but there was a sort of indolence in the air, a reluctance to get back into the swing of everyday life. It would have been easier if it had rained or if the weather had been cold. This year, summer was refusing to die.

The driver turned around as they left Rue Dareau, close to the railway embankment.

'What number?'

'I don't know. It's a packaging company . . .'

Another bend and they spotted a large concrete building with curtainless windows. Along the entire length of the façade were the words:

Jouane & Goulet Packaging
Formerly Josselin Packaging

'Shall I wait for you?'

'Yes.'

There were two doors, one to the factory and the other, further along, to the offices. Maigret went in through this door and found himself in very modern premises.

'Can I help you?'

A girl popped her head through a window and looked at him with curiosity. Admittedly, Maigret's face wore a frown, as was customary during the early stages of an investigation, and he was gazing slowly about him as if making an inventory of the place.

'Who's the head of the company?'

'Monsieur Jouane and Monsieur Goulet,' she replied as if that were obvious.

'I know. But which one's the boss?'

'It depends. Monsieur Jouane is mainly in charge of the design side, and Monsieur Goulet of production and sales.'

'Are they both here?'

'Monsieur Goulet is still on holiday. What is it you want?'

'To see Monsieur Jouane.'

'Who's asking?'

'Detective Chief Inspector Maigret.'

'Do you have an appointment?'

'No.'

'Just a moment . . .'

She went to the back of her glassed-in cubicle and spoke to a young woman in a white coat, who darted an inquisitive look at the visitor then left the room.

'My colleague's gone to fetch him. He's on the factory floor.'

Maigret could hear the sound of machinery. When a

side door opened, he glimpsed a vast workshop where other girls and women in white worked in rows, as on a production line.

'You were asking for me?'

The man must have been around forty-five. He was tall, with an open face, and he also wore a white coat, which was unbuttoned, revealing a well-cut suit.

'Please come this way . . .'

They climbed a light oak staircase, passing a window through which he saw half a dozen draughtsmen hunched over their work.

Another door and they were in a sunny office, with a secretary typing away in a corner.

'Leave us, Mademoiselle Blanche.'

He motioned to Maigret to have a seat and then sat down at his desk, surprised and slightly anxious.

'I wonder . . .' he began.

'Have you heard about Monsieur Josselin's death?'

'What? Monsieur Josselin is dead? When did that happen? Is he back from his holiday?'

'You haven't seen him since his return from La Baule?'

'No. He hasn't been to see us yet. Did he have a heart attack?'

'He was murdered.'

'Josselin?'

It was clear that Jouane struggled to take it in.

'It's not possible. Who would have . . .?'

'He was killed at his home yesterday evening, with two shots from a revolver.'

'By whom?'

'That's what I'm trying to find out, Monsieur Jouane.'

'Wasn't his wife with him?'

'She was at the theatre with her daughter.'

Jouane bowed his head, visibly shocked.

'Poor man . . . It's so hard to believe . . .'

And then he grew indignant.

'But who could have gained . . . Listen, inspector . . . You didn't know him . . . He was the best man in the world . . . He was a father to me, more than a father . . . When I started here, I was sixteen and I knew nothing . . . My father had just died . . . My mother was a cleaner . . . I began as a delivery boy on a tricycle . . . Monsieur Josselin taught me everything . . . Later, he made me a manager . . . And when he decided to retire from business, he called us into his office, Goulet and myself . . . Goulet had started out working on the machines . . .'

'He told us that his doctor had advised him to work less, but he couldn't do that. Coming here two or three hours a day like a dilettante was unthinkable for a man like him, who was used to dealing with everything and who stayed late almost every evening, long after the machines had stopped.'

'Were you afraid of seeing an outsider become your new boss?'

'I admit I was. For Goulet and for me, this news was a real disaster, and we looked at each other in dismay while Monsieur Josselin smiled mischievously . . . Do you know what he did?'

'I was told last night.'

'Who told you?'

'His doctor.'

'Naturally, we both had some savings, but not enough to buy a business like this . . . Monsieur Josselin had his notary come in and they found a way to hand over the firm by staggering the payments over a long period . . . A period which, of course, is far from over . . . To be honest, there's another twenty-five years to run . . .'

'Did he still come here from time to time?'

'He visited us discreetly, as if he were afraid of getting in our way. He made sure that everything was going well, that we were happy, and when we asked him for advice, he gave it as if he didn't feel it was his place to do so.'

'Do you know if he had any enemies?'

'He had none! He wasn't the sort of man to make enemies. Everyone loved him. Go into the offices, on to the shop floor, ask anyone what they thought of him—'

'Are you married, Monsieur Jouane?'

'Yes. I have three children and we live near Versailles, in a house I had built . . .'

He too was a good man! Was Maigret only going to come across good people in this investigation? He was almost irritated by it because, after all, on the one hand there was a dead man, and on the other, a man who had shot René Josselin twice.

'Did you often go to Rue Notre-Dame-des-Champs?'

'I went there four or five times altogether . . . No! I'm forgetting that five years ago, when Monsieur Josselin had a bad dose of flu, I would go there every morning to take him his post and receive his instructions.'

'Did you ever have dinner or lunch there?'

'Goulet and I had dinner there with our wives the evening we signed the contract, when Monsieur Josselin handed over the business.'

'What kind of man is Goulet?'

'A technician, a hard worker.'

'How old?'

'About the same age as me. We started work here one year apart.'

'Where is he at the moment?'

'On the Île de Ré, with his wife and children.'

'How many does he have?'

'Three, like me.'

'What do you think of Madame Josselin?'

'I barely know her. She seems like an excellent woman. A different kind of person from her husband.'

'What do you mean?'

'That she's a bit more aloof . . .'

'What about their daughter?'

'She'd sometimes drop in to see her father at the office, but we had little contact with her.'

'I presume that René Josselin's death makes no difference to your financial arrangements?'

'I haven't considered that yet . . . Wait . . . No . . . There's no reason . . . Instead of paying the sums due to him directly, we'll pay them to his heirs . . . To Madame Josselin, I suppose.'

'Are they large sums?'

'It varies from one year to the next, because the arrangement includes profit sharing . . . In any case, there's enough to live very well . . .'

'Do you consider that the Josselins lived very well?'

'They had a good life. They had a beautiful apartment, a car, a house in La Baule . . .'

'But they could have lived more lavishly?'

Jouane thought it over.

'Yes . . . Of course . . .'

'Was Josselin tight-fisted?'

'He wouldn't have come up with the arrangement he offered Goulet and myself if he'd been mean . . . No . . . I think he lived as he wanted to live, you know . . . He didn't have extravagant tastes . . . He preferred peace and quiet above all.'

'What about Madame Josselin?'

'She likes looking after her home, her daughter, and now her grandchildren.'

'How did the Josselins react to their daughter's marriage?'

'It's difficult for me to say . . . . All that didn't happen here but at Rue Notre-Dame-des-Champs . . . It's obvious that Monsieur Josselin adored Mademoiselle Véronique and that it was hard for him to let her go . . . I have a daughter too . . . She's twelve . . . I confess I dread the day when a stranger will take her from me and she'll no longer bear my name . . . I suppose it's the same for all fathers, isn't it?'

'The fact that his son-in-law was penniless . . .'

'That's more likely something that would have pleased him.'

'What about Madame Josselin?'

'I'm not so sure . . . The idea that her daughter was marrying the son of a postman—'

'Fabre's father is a postman . . .'

'In Melun or in a village around there . . . I'm telling you what I know . . . Apparently he did all his degrees with the help of scholarships . . . They also say that, if he wanted to, he could soon be one of the youngest professors at the faculty of medicine.'

'One more question, Monsieur Jouane. I fear it may shock you after what you have just told me. Did Monsieur Josselin have one or several mistresses? Was he a skirt chaser?'

Just as Jouane opened his mouth, Maigret interrupted him.

'I imagine that since getting married, you have occasionally slept with a woman other than your wife?'

'I've had occasion to, yes. While avoiding any kind of relationship. You understand what I mean? I wouldn't want to jeopardize our family life.'

'There are a lot of young women working all around you—'

'Not them. Never. It's a matter of principle. Besides, it would be risky.'

'Thank you for your honesty. You consider yourself to be a normal man. René Josselin was a normal man too. He married late, at around thirty-five . . .'

'I understand what you mean . . . I'm trying to visualize Monsieur Josselin in that situation . . . but I can't . . . I don't know why . . . I know he was a man like any other . . . but even so . . .'

'You weren't aware of him having any affairs?'

'No . . . I never saw him ogling any of our women

workers either, even though some of them are very pretty . . . Some must even have tried it on, as they did with me . . . No, inspector, I don't think you'll find anything of that nature.'

Abruptly he asked:

'How come there's nothing about it in the newspapers?'

'The press will be reporting it this afternoon.'

Maigret rose with a sigh.

'Thank you, Monsieur Jouane. If you remember any little detail that might be helpful, telephone me.'

'As far as I'm concerned, it's an inexplicable crime . . .'

Maigret almost grunted:

'For me too.'

Except that he knew that there weren't any inexplicable crimes. People don't kill without a strong reason.

And, pushed a little further, he might have added:

'People don't just kill randomly.'

Because his experience had taught him that some individuals are destined to be victims.

'Do you know when the funeral will be?'

'The body will be returned to the family only after the autopsy.'

'Has that not taken place yet?'

'It's probably underway as we speak.'

'I must telephone Goulet right away . . . He's not due back until next week.'

Maigret gave a little wave to the girl in her glass cage, wondering why she stifled a giggle as she watched him walk past.

3.

The street was quiet, provincial, with one side in the sun and the other in the shade. Two dogs were sniffing each other in the middle of the road, and through the open windows women could be seen going about their housework. Three Little Sisters of the Poor, with their wide skirts and the wings of their cornettes fluttering like birds, were walking in the direction of the Luxembourg Gardens and Maigret watched them from a distance, his mind a blank. Then he frowned on spotting a uniformed police officer trying to fend off half a dozen reporters and photographers outside the Josselins' apartment building.

He was used to it and shouldn't have been surprised. He had just told Jouane that the afternoon papers were bound to report on the case. René Josselin had been murdered and people who have been murdered automatically become public property. In a few hours' time, every detail of a family's private life, true or false, would be laid bare, and everyone would be entitled to speculate. Why all of a sudden did this shock him? He was annoyed with himself for being shocked. He felt as if he had been sucked into the bourgeois, almost edifying, atmosphere that surrounded those people, 'good people', so everyone kept telling him.

The photographers snapped away as he stepped out of

the taxi and the reporters crowded round him while he paid the driver.

'What's your opinion, inspector?'

He brushed them aside, muttering:

'When I have something to tell you, I'll call you. There are women grieving up there and it would be more considerate to leave them in peace.'

But he himself was not going to leave them in peace. He greeted the uniformed officer and went inside the building, which he was seeing in daylight for the first time. It was very cheerful, very bright.

He was about to walk past the concierge's lodge, with its white net curtain hanging on the inside of the glazed door, but he changed his mind, rapped on the glass and turned the knob.

The lodge consisted of a small living room with polished furniture and was typical of the sort that are attached to apartment buildings in affluent neighbourhoods. A voice asked:

'Who is it?'

'Detective Chief Inspector Maigret.'

'Come in, inspector.'

The voice hailed from a kitchen with white walls where the concierge, her arms bare to the elbows and a white pinafore over her black dress, was busy sterilizing feeding bottles.

She was young and affable, and her figure still had the soft plumpness of her recent pregnancy. Pointing to a door, she said quietly:

'Not too loud, my husband's asleep.'

Maigret recalled that the husband was a police officer and that he'd been on duty the night before.

'I've been besieged by reporters all morning, and some of them went upstairs when I had my back turned. My husband ended up informing the police station and they sent one of his colleagues over.'

The baby was asleep in a wicker cradle trimmed with yellow flounces.

'Have you any news?' she asked.

He shook his head.

'I suppose you're certain, aren't you?' he asked quietly. 'No one went out last night after Doctor Fabre had left?'

'No one, inspector. As I said again earlier to one of your men, a fat officer with a ruddy face, Inspector Torrence, I think. He spent over an hour in the building, questioning the residents. Not many of them are here at the moment. Some are still on holiday. The Tuplers aren't back from America. The place is half empty.'

'How long have you been working here?'

'Six years. I took over from one of my aunts, who'd been the concierge for forty years.'

'Did the Josselins entertain a lot?'

'Very rarely. They're quiet people, pleasant to everyone, and they live a very routine life. Doctor Larue and his wife came to dinner from time to time. And the Josselins would go over to them for dinner too.'

Like the Maigrets and the Pardons. Maigret wondered whether they too had a set day.

'In the morning, at around nine, while Madame Manu did the cleaning, Monsieur Josselin would go out for his walk. He was so regular that I could have set the clock by him. He'd pop into the lodge, say something about the weather and pick up his post. After glancing at the envelopes, he'd slip them into his pocket and then he'd slowly make his way to the Luxembourg Gardens. He always walked at the same gentle pace.'

'Did he receive a lot of post?'

'Not a lot. Later, at around ten, while he was still out, his wife would come down, all dressed up, even to go shopping. I've never seen her go out without a hat.'

'What time did her husband return home?'

'It depended on the weather. If it was sunny, not before eleven thirty or twelve. When it rained, he didn't stay out so long, but he still went for his walk.'

'What about the afternoons?'

She had finished replacing the tops on the bottles, which she put away in the refrigerator.

'The two of them would go out together, but no more than once or twice a week. Madame Fabre also visited them. Before the birth of her second child, she sometimes brought the eldest one with her.'

'Has she always got on well with her mother?'

'Yes, I think so. They often go to the theatre together, as they did yesterday.'

'Recently, have you noticed any letters in a different handwriting from the usual correspondence?'

'No.'

'And no one called on Monsieur Josselin when he was at home alone, for example?'

'No. I was thinking about all that during the night

because I was expecting you to ask me those questions. You see, inspector, they are people about whom there is nothing to tell . . .'

'Did they socialize with any of the other residents?'

'Not to my knowledge. In Paris, it's rare for the residents of an apartment building to know one another, except in the working-class districts. Everyone lives their life unaware of their next-door neighbours.'

'Has Madame Fabre returned?'

'A few minutes ago.'

'Thank you.'

The lift stopped at the third floor where there were two doors. In front of each one was a large doormat with a red border. He rang the left-hand bell, heard muffled footsteps and, after a brief hesitation, the door opened a crack, allowing only a sliver of light through, because the chain had not been taken off.

'What is it?' asked an unfriendly voice.

'Detective Chief Inspector Maigret.'

A face with strong features, belonging to a woman in her fifties, peered out to look the visitor up and down suspiciously.

'All right! I believe you! There were so many reporters this morning . . .'

She took off the chain and Maigret saw the apartment as it normally was, with every object in its place, and sunshine streaming in through the two windows.

'If it's Madame Josselin you wish to see . . .'

He had been shown into the drawing room, where there was no trace of the previous night's events or mess.

A door opened immediately and Véronique, wearing a navy-blue suit, took two steps into the room.

She was visibly tired, and Maigret noticed a slight hesitation, a searching, in her eyes. When her gaze rested on an object or on her visitor's face, it seemed to be looking for a support, or the answer to a question.

'You haven't found anything?' she murmured despondently.

'How is your mother?'

'I have only just come back. I went to see my children and to change my clothes. I think I told you over the telephone. I don't remember. I'm losing track. Mother slept. When she woke up, she didn't speak. She drank a cup of coffee but refused to eat. I wanted her to stay in bed, but I couldn't persuade her and now she's getting dressed.'

She looked about her again, avoiding the armchair where her father had died. The chess game was no longer on the pedestal table. A half-smoked cigar, which Maigret had noticed the previous night, had disappeared.

'Your mother said absolutely nothing?'

'She only answers yes or no. She's perfectly lucid. It seems she's only got one thing on her mind. Is it her that you came to see?'

'If possible . . .'

'She'll be ready in a few minutes. Don't push her too much, I beg of you. Everyone takes her for a calm woman, because she's always so self-possessed. But I know that she is obsessively anxious. Only she doesn't show it.'

'Have you often seen her in the grip of a powerful emotion?'

'It depends what you call powerful. When I was a child, for example, I would sometimes exasperate her, as all children can exasperate their parents. Instead of slapping me, or getting angry, she'd turn pale and seem unable to speak. At those times, almost always, she'd lock herself in her room and that really frightened me.'

'What about your father?'

'My father never lost his temper. His response was to smile as if making fun of me.'

'Is your husband at the hospital?'

'Since seven o'clock this morning. I left my children with the maid because I didn't want to risk bringing them with me. I don't know what we're going to do. I don't like leaving mother alone in the apartment. There's no room at our place, and besides, she'd refuse to come.'

'Couldn't the cleaner, Madame Manu, spend the night here?'

'No! She has a grown-up son of twenty-four who's even more demanding than a husband and gets angry whenever she dares return home late . . . We'll have to find someone, perhaps a nurse . . . Mother will make a fuss . . . Of course, I'll spend as much time here as I can . . .'

Although she had regular features and reddish-blonde hair, she wasn't particularly attractive because she lacked any spark.

'I think I can hear mother . . .'

The door opened and Maigret was surprised to see before him a woman who still appeared very youthful. He knew that she was fifteen years younger than her husband, but he had still expected to see a grandmotherly figure.

Yet her body, in a very simple black dress, was more girlish than her daughter's. She had chestnut hair and bright, almost black eyes. Despite the tragedy, despite her state, she was impeccably made up and nothing in her appearance was out of place.

'Detective Chief Inspector Maigret,' he introduced himself.

She fluttered her eyelashes, gazed about her and ended up looking at Véronique, who immediately mumbled:

'Would you rather I left the room?'

Maigret said neither yes nor no. The mother didn't stop her. Véronique slipped noiselessly out of the room. All the comings and goings in the apartment were muffled by the thick carpeting on which antique rugs were scattered.

'Do sit down,' said René Josselin's widow, who remained standing beside her husband's armchair.

Maigret hesitated and finally took a seat. Madame Josselin went over and sat in her armchair beside the sewing cabinet. She refrained from leaning against the chair back, holding herself bolt upright as convent-educated women do. Her lips were thin, probably because of her age, and her hands were slender but still beautiful.

'I apologize for being here, Madame Josselin, and I confess I don't know what questions to ask. I am mindful of your distress, your grief.'

She gazed at him unflinchingly, and he wondered whether she heard his words or whether she was listening to her own internal monologue.

'Your husband was the victim of a seemingly

inexplicable crime and I am obliged to leave no stone unturned in trying to get to the bottom of it.'

Her head made a very slight nodding movement, as if she were agreeing with him.

'You were at the Théâtre de la Madeleine last night, with your daughter. It is likely that the person who killed your husband knew he would find him on his own. When was the outing arranged?'

She replied reticently:

'Three or four days ago. I think it was Saturday or Sunday.'

'Whose idea was it?'

'Mine. I was curious about the play, which received a lot of good reviews.'

He was surprised to hear her speaking with such calm precision, knowing what condition she had still been in at four o'clock that morning.

'My daughter and I discussed the outing and she telephoned her husband to ask if he would be joining us.'

'Did the three of you sometimes go out together?'

'Rarely. My son-in-law is only interested in medicine and his patients.'

'What about your husband?'

'He and I would go to the cinema or the music hall from time to time. He loved music hall.'

Her voice was flat, without warmth. She reeled off her answers, staring at Maigret's face as if he were an examiner.

'Did you make the reservations over the telephone?'

'Yes. Seats 97 and 99. I remember, because I always insist on being next to the central aisle.'

'Who knew that you would be out that evening?'

'My husband, my son-in-law and the cleaner.'

'No one else?'

'My hairdresser, because I went to his salon in the afternoon.'

'Did your husband smoke?'

Maigret was jumping from one idea to the next and he had just remembered the cigar in the ashtray.

'Not much. A cigar after each meal. Sometimes he'd smoke one during his morning walk.'

'Forgive me for this ridiculous question, but do you know of any enemies he might have had?'

She did not let out a volley of protestations but merely said:

'No.'

'He never gave you the impression he was hiding something, that he had some sort of secret life?'

'No.'

'What did you think when you found him dead on your return last night?'

She appeared to swallow hard and said:

'That he was dead.'

Her face had become sterner, even more set, and Maigret thought for a moment that her eyes were going to mist over.

'You didn't ask yourself who had killed him?'

He thought he sensed an imperceptible hesitation.

'No.'

'Why did you not telephone the police straight away?'

She didn't reply immediately but looked away from Maigret briefly.

'I don't know.'

'You called your son-in-law first?'

'I didn't call anyone. It was Véronique who telephoned home, anxious at not finding her husband here.'

'Was she surprised not to find him there either?'

'I don't know.'

'Who thought of Doctor Larue?'

'I think it was me. We needed someone to take care of what needed to be done.'

'You have no suspicions, Madame Josselin?'

'None.'

'Why did you get up this morning?'

'Because I had no reason to stay in bed.'

'Are you certain that nothing's been stolen?'

'My daughter checked. She knows where everything is as well as I do. Apart from the revolver . . .'

'When was the last time you saw it?'

'A few days ago. I'm not exactly sure.'

'Did you know it was loaded?'

'Yes. My husband has always had a loaded revolver in the house. In the early days of our marriage, he used to keep it in his bedside drawer. Then, for fear Véronique might touch it, and because there were no drawers that locked in the bedroom, he kept it in the drawing room. For a long time, that drawer was kept locked. Now that Véronique is an adult and married . . .'

'Did your husband seem to be afraid of something?'

'No.'

'Did he keep a lot of money in the apartment?'

'Very little. We pay for nearly everything by cheque.'

'Did you ever, on coming home, find someone you didn't know with your husband?'

'No.'

'And you have never come across your husband with a stranger either?'

'No, inspector.'

'Thank you . . .'

Maigret felt hot. He had just carried out one of the most painful interrogations of his career. It was like throwing a ball that doesn't bounce back. He had the impression that his questions hadn't hit home, that they hadn't pierced the surface, and that the answers he received were neutral and lifeless.

She hadn't avoided any of the questions, but nor had she uttered any personal comment.

She didn't get up to say goodbye but remained upright in her armchair, and he was unable to read anything in her eyes, even though they were very animated.

'I apologize for this intrusion.'

She didn't protest but waited until he was on his feet before rising to follow him as he made his way awkwardly towards the door.

'If anything occurs to you, a recollection, a suspicion of any kind . . .'

Once again, she replied with a flutter of her eyelashes.

'A police officer is standing guard by the door and I hope you won't be bothered by the press.'

'Madame Manu told me they'd come already.'

'Have you known her long?'

'Around six months.'

'Does she have a key to the apartment?'

'I had one cut for her, yes.'

'Who else had a key?'

'My husband and I. Our daughter too. She still has the key she used when she lived at home.'

'Is that all?'

'Yes. There's a fifth key, which I call the emergency key, that I keep in my dressing table.'

'Is it still there?'

'I've just seen it.'

'May I ask your daughter a question?'

Madame Josselin went and opened a door, disappeared for a moment and returned with Véronique Fabre, who looked from one to the other.

'Your mother tells me that you still have a key to the apartment. I'd like to ascertain that you still have it . . .'

She went over to a chest of drawers on which a blue leather handbag sat. She opened it and took out a small, flat key.

'Did you have it with you at the theatre, yesterday?'

'No. I had an evening bag, much smaller than this one, and I took hardly anything with me.'

'So, you left your key in your apartment on Boulevard Brune?'

That was all. He couldn't think of any more questions he could decently ask. Besides, he was in a hurry to leave that hushed world which made him feel ill at ease.'

'Thank you.'

He walked down the stairs to stretch his legs and, as soon as he rounded the first bend, let out a deep sigh.

There were no reporters on the pavement outside, where the police officer was slowly pacing back and forth. They'd congregated at the counter of a small bar opposite, and now they rushed over to Maigret.

'Did you question the two women?'

He looked at them in a similar way as the widow, as if he didn't see their faces but was looking through them.

'Is it true that Madame Josselin is indisposed and refuses to answer?'

'I have nothing to say to you, gentlemen.'

'When do you hope . . .?'

He gave a dismissive wave and headed towards Boulevard Raspail in search of a taxi. Since the reporters hadn't followed him but had resumed their vigil, he was able to stop off at the same bar as the previous night and drink a beer.

It was almost midday when he walked into his office at Quai des Orfèvres. A moment later, he half-opened the door to the inspectors' room and spotted Lapointe and Torrence.

'Come into my office, both of you.'

He sat down heavily at his desk, selected the fattest of his pipes, and proceeded to fill it.

'What have you been doing?' he asked young Lapointe.

'I went to Rue Julie to do some cross-checking. I questioned the three concierges and they all confirm that last night someone came asking if there was a sick child in their building. One of them was suspicious, because she thought the man looked quite scruffy and didn't seem like a real doctor. She nearly called the police.'

'What time was that?'

'Between ten thirty and eleven.'

'What about at the hospital?'

'That was trickier. I arrived at a busy time, when the consultant and the doctors were doing their ward rounds. Everyone's on red alert. I spotted Doctor Fabre from a distance, and I'm certain he recognized me.'

'He didn't react?'

'No. There were several of them in white coats and skullcaps, following the big boss.'

'Does he often drop in to the hospital in the evening?'

'Apparently they all do, either when there's an emergency or when they're in charge of a serious case. Doctor Fabre is the one who does so most frequently. I managed to collar a couple of nurses. They all speak of him in the same way. At the hospital, he's seen as a sort of saint . . .'

'Did he stay at the bedside of his young patient all the while he was there?'

'No. He went into several wards and chatted for some time with a junior doctor.'

'Do they know, at the hospital?'

'I don't think so. People gave me strange looks. Especially the young woman who must be more than a nurse – an assistant, I suppose. She said to me angrily: "If you have indiscreet questions to ask, then ask Doctor Fabre himself."'

'Has the pathologist called?'

After an autopsy, the pathologist habitually called Quai des Orfèvres before sending the official report, which always took a while to produce.

'He recovered the two bullets. One was in the aorta and would have been sufficient to kill Josselin.'

'What time does he think the murder took place?'

'As far as he can tell, between nine and eleven in the evening. Doctor Ledent would like to know what time Josselin had his last meal, to help him pinpoint the time more accurately.'

'Phone the cleaner and ask her, and let him know the answer.'

Meanwhile, big Torrence was standing by the window watching the boats going past on the Seine.

'What shall I do now?' asked Lapointe.

'First of all, make that telephone call. Now then, Torrence . . .'

He was more formal towards Torrence, even though he'd known him longer than Lapointe, who looked more like a young student than a police inspector.

'How did you get on with the residents?'

'Here's a plan of the building for you. It will make things easier.'

He put it on the desk, stood behind Maigret and from time to time pointed at one of the boxes he'd drawn.

'First of all, the ground floor. You probably know that the concierge's husband is a police officer and that he was on night duty, but his beat didn't take him past the building. He came home at seven in the morning.'

'And then . . .'

'On the left lives a spinster, Mademoiselle Nolan, who's said to be very wealthy and very stingy. She watched television until eleven and then went to bed. She didn't hear anything, and no one knocked on her door.'

'On the right?'

'A certain Davey. He lives alone too, a widower; he's the assistant manager of an insurance company. He had dinner in town, as he does every evening, and returned home at nine fifteen. From what I've learned, an attractive young woman occasionally comes and keeps him company, but that was not the case yesterday. He read the newspapers and fell asleep at around ten thirty without hearing anything out of the ordinary. It was only when the men from the forensics team came into the building with their equipment that he was roused. He got up and asked the officer on duty what was going on.'

'What was his reaction?'

'Nothing. He went back to bed.'

'Did he know the Josselins?'

'Only by sight. First floor right is the Aresco family. There are six or seven of them, all dark-haired and fat. The women are quite pretty, and they all speak with a strong accent. There's the father, the mother, a sister-in-law, an older girl of twenty and two or three children. They didn't go out yesterday.'

'Are you sure? The concierge says—'

'I know. She told me too. Someone came in shortly after the doctor left and shouted "Aresco" as they passed the lodge . . . Monsieur Aresco is furious . . . The entire family played cards and they swear no one went out of the apartment.'

'What does the concierge say about that?'

'She's almost certain that's the name she was given, and she even thought she recognized the accent.'

'*Almost certain . . .*' repeated Maigret. '*She thought she recognized . . .* What do the Arescos do?'

'They have a large business in South America, where they live for part of the year. They also have a home in Switzerland. They were still there two weeks ago.'

'Do they know the Josselins?'

'They claim they didn't even know the name.'

'Go on.'

'On the right, opposite them, is an art critic, Joseph Mérillon, currently away on a government mission in Athens.'

'On the second floor?'

'The entire floor is occupied by the Tuplers, who are in the United States right now.'

'No servants?'

'The apartment is locked up for three months. The carpets have been sent to be cleaned.'

'Third floor?'

'No one home last night next door to the Josselins. The Delilles, a middle-aged couple whose children are married, stay on the Riviera until the beginning of October. These people take long holidays, chief.'

'Fourth floor?'

'Above the Josselins are the Meurats, an architect, his wife and their twelve-year-old daughter. They didn't go out. The architect worked until midnight and didn't hear anything. His window was open. Opposite them, an industrialist and his wife, the Blanchons, who left the same day to go hunting in Sologne. On the fifth floor is another woman on her own, Madame Schwartz, who often has a woman friend visit in the evenings but not yesterday, and she went to bed early. Lastly, there's a young couple, married last month, on holiday in the Nièvre at the wife's parents' place. On the sixth floor, there are only servants' rooms.'

Maigret looked at the plan glumly. Admittedly, some boxes were empty – people who were still by the sea, in the country or abroad.

Even so, half of the building had been occupied the previous night. Residents playing cards, watching television, reading or sleeping. One was still up working. The concierge hadn't gone back to sleep properly after Doctor Fabre had left.

And yet, two shots had been fired and a man had been killed in one of the boxes without the day-to-day routine of the others being disrupted.

'Good people . . .'

All of them were probably also good people, whose activities were known and whose lives were comfortable and without secrets.

Had the concierge, after letting Doctor Fabre out, fallen into a deeper sleep than she realized? There was no doubt she had spoken in good faith. She was an intelligent woman, who was perfectly aware of the importance of her words.

She stated that someone had come in between ten thirty and eleven and shouted the Arescos' name in passing.

But the Arescos swore that no one had left or entered their apartment that evening. They didn't know the Josselins. It was plausible. No one in the building took any notice of their neighbours, as is often the case in Paris, especially among the upper middle classes.

'I wonder why a resident returning home would have given another resident's name . . .'

'And supposing it wasn't someone who lived there?'

'According to the concierge, they wouldn't have been able to leave without being seen.'

Maigret frowned.

'It sounds stupid,' he grumbled. 'But logically, that's the only explanation possible . . .'

'That the person remained in the building?'

'Until this morning, at any rate . . . During the day, it must be easy to come and go unnoticed.'

'Do you mean that the murderer could have been there, very close to the police officers, during the deputy public prosecutor's visit and while the forensics team were at work in the apartment?'

'There are empty apartments . . . Take a locksmith with you and check whether any of the locks have been forced.'

'I presume I don't go inside?'

'No, just check the locks from the outside.'

'Is that all?'

'For now. What would you want to do?'

Big Torrence looked thoughtful and concluded:

'True . . .'

A crime had definitely taken place, because a man had

been killed. Only it wasn't a crime like any other, because the victim wasn't a victim like any other.

'A good man!' echoed Maigret with a sort of anger.

Who could have had a reason to kill that good man?

It wouldn't take much for him to start loathing good people.

4.

Maigret returned home for lunch. Sitting by the open window, he noticed a particular gesture of his wife's, even though she made it every day. She would remove her apron before sitting down to eat, and often, immediately afterwards, she'd fluff up her hair.

They too could have a maid. It was Madame Maigret who had never wanted one, saying she'd feel useless if she didn't have her housework to do. She agreed to have a cleaner come only two or three times a week to do the heavy housework, and even then, she sometimes did the job again herself.

Was the same true of Madame Josselin? Doubtless not exactly. She was meticulous, as the state of the apartment showed, but she probably didn't feel the need to do everything with her own hands, as Madame Maigret would.

Why, as he ate, was he comparing the two women, who had nothing whatsoever in common?

In Rue Notre-Dame-des-Champs, Madame Josselin and her daughter would be eating in privacy, and Maigret imagined that they must be covertly watching one another. Might they be discussing practical details?

Meanwhile, back at Boulevard Brune, Doctor Fabre, if he'd gone back home, which was likely, was alone with his children. He only had a young maid to look after them and do all the housework. He would bolt down his lunch before returning to his surgery, where the procession of young patients and anxious mothers would continue all afternoon without a break. Had he found someone to stay at Rue Notre-Dame-des-Champs with his mother-in-law? Would she agree to having a stranger living with her?

Maigret caught himself worrying about these things as if they were members of his own family. René Josselin was dead, and it wasn't just a matter of finding his murderer. Little by little, those who were left behind would have to reorganize their lives.

He would have liked to pay a visit to Boulevard Brune to get a feel for the surroundings in which Fabre lived with his wife and children. He'd been told that they were in a new building near the Cité Universitaire, and he pictured one of those anonymous apartment blocks he had seen in passing, and which he would readily have called a people hutch. A bare white façade, already grimy. Rows of uniform windows and identical apartments from top to bottom, the bathrooms one above the other, the kitchens too, and walls so thin that every sound could be heard.

He would have sworn that the atmosphere there wasn't as orderly as in Rue Notre-Dame-des-Champs, that life was less regulated, with meals at odd times, and that this was as much to do with Fabre's character as with his wife's lackadaisical attitude or perhaps her incompetence.

She had been a spoiled child. Her mother still came to see her almost every day, looked after the children, took the eldest one out for walks. Did she not also try to put a little order into a life which she must consider too bohemian?

Did the two women at the table realize that, logically, the only suspect at this point of the investigation was Paul Fabre? He was the last person known to have been alone with Josselin.

Admittedly he couldn't have made the telephone call asking him to go to Rue Julie, but at the hospital there were plenty of people who were devoted to him and would do him a favour. And he knew where the revolver was kept.

And it could be argued that he had a motive. True, he wasn't interested in money. Had it not been for his father-in-law, he would never have burdened himself with a private practice but would have dedicated all his time to the hospital where he must feel more at home than anywhere else.

But what about Véronique? Could she be starting to regret marrying a man universally acclaimed as a saint? Did she not wish for a different life? Did not her mood at home suggest her discontent?

After Josselin's death, the Fabres would doubtless receive their share of the inheritance.

Maigret tried to imagine the scene: the two men sitting at the chess board, silent and serious, like all chess players; the doctor, at some point, getting up and going over to the chest where the automatic lay in a drawer . . .

He shook his head. It didn't stack up. He couldn't picture Fabre walking towards his father-in-law with his finger on the trigger.

Had an argument, a quarrel turned nasty and ended up with the pair of them blowing a fuse?

No matter how hard he tried, he couldn't see it. It didn't fit with the two men's temperaments.

Besides, there was the mysterious visitor the concierge had mentioned who'd shouted 'Aresco'.

'I had a phone call from Francine Pardon,' said Madame Maigret all of a sudden, perhaps deliberately to take his mind off things.

He was so far away that, at first, he just stared at her blankly.

'They came back from Italy on Monday. Do you remember how much they were looking forward to going away just the two of them?'

It was the first time that the Pardons were holidaying on their own for more than twenty years. They had gone by car with the intention of visiting Florence, Rome and Naples, and returning via Venice and Milan, stopping wherever the fancy took them.

'They've invited us for dinner next Wednesday, as a matter of fact.'

'Why not?'

Had it not become a tradition? The dinner should have been on the first Wednesday of the month but had been postponed because of the holidays.

'Apparently the trip was exhausting. The traffic on the roads was as bad as on the Champs-Élysées and they spent an hour or two every night trying to find a hotel room.'

'How's their daughter?'

'Well. The baby's a delight . . .'

Madame Pardon too went almost every afternoon to visit her daughter, who had got married the previous year and now had a baby that was a few months old.

If the Maigrets had had a child, he or she would be married now, and like the other women, Madame Maigret . . .

'Do you know what they've decided?'

'No.'

'To buy a little house by the sea or in the country, so they can spend the holidays with their daughter, their son-in-law and the child . . .'

The Josselins had a house in La Baule. They lived there one month a year with their family, perhaps more. René Josselin had retired.

It suddenly struck Maigret. The packaging manufacturer had been an active man all his life, spending most of his time in Rue du Saint-Gothard and often working late into the evening.

He only saw his wife at mealtimes and during part of the evening.

Because a heart attack had given him a sudden scare, he'd handed over his business almost at once.

What would he, Maigret, do if he retired and found himself with his wife all day? It was already decided, because they were planning to live in the country and they had already bought their house.

But what if he had to stay in Paris?

Each morning, Josselin went out at a set time, around nine, as if leaving for the office. According to the concierge, he headed for the Luxembourg Gardens, with the regular, cautious step of someone with a heart condition.

The Josselins didn't have a dog, and that surprised Maigret. He could picture René Josselin walking his dog on a lead. There wasn't a cat in the apartment either.

He bought the newspapers. Did he sit on a bench in the gardens to read them? Did he ever enter into a conversation with one of his neighbours? Was he in the habit of meeting the same person, man or woman?

Maigret had instructed Lapointe to go to Rue Notre-Dame-des-Champs and ask for a photograph of Josselin, and then to question the local traders and the Luxembourg Gardens park keepers on the off chance, to try and piece together the victim's morning movements.

Would that yield any results? He preferred not to think about it. The man was dead. He had never seen him alive, and he was becoming obsessed with this family, whose existence he had been unaware of the previous day.

'Will you be coming home for dinner?'

'I think so. I hope so.'

He went to wait for his bus at the corner of Boulevard Richard-Lenoir. He stayed outside on the bus platform, smoking his pipe and looking about him at the men and women leading their ordinary lives as if the Josselins didn't exist and as if there wasn't, in Paris, a man who for some unfathomable reason had killed another.

Once in his office, he threw himself into tedious paperwork to avoid having to think about the case, and he must have succeeded because, at around three o'clock, he was surprised, on answering the telephone, to hear Torrence's excited voice.

'I'm still in the neighbourhood, chief . . .'

He almost asked:

'What neighbourhood?'

'I thought it better to phone you than to return to the

office because you might decide to come yourself . . . I've discovered something—'

'Are the two women still in their apartment?'

'All three. Madame Manu's there too.'

'What's happened?'

'We brought in a locksmith and examined all the doors, including the ones that open on to the backstairs. None of them look as if they've been forced. We didn't stop at the fifth floor. We went up to the sixth, where the maids' rooms are.'

'What did you find?'

'Hold on. Most of them were locked. As we were bending over one of the locks, the next door opened a crack and we were amazed to see a young woman stark naked. She wasn't embarrassed at all but stared at us curiously. A beautiful girl, by the way, dark-haired, with huge eyes, a very pronounced Spanish or South American type.'

Maigret waited, and did a doodle of a woman's torso on his blotting pad.

'I asked her what she was doing there, and she answered in poor French that it was her hour off and that she was the Arescos' maid.

'"Why are you trying to open that door?" she asked suspiciously.

'And she added, without sounding alarmed at the thought: "Are you thieves?"

'I told her who we were. She didn't know that one of the residents had been killed during the night.

'"The kind, fat gentleman who always smiled at me on the stairs?"

'Then she said:

'"It's not their new maid, I hope?"'

'I didn't understand. We must have looked ridiculous and I felt like asking her to put some clothes on.

'"What new maid?"'

'"They must have a new maid, because I heard a noise in the room last night . . ."'

Maigret abruptly stopped doodling. He was furious not to have thought of it. To be more exact, he had started to think of it the previous night. There had been a moment when an idea had begun forming in his mind and he'd felt he was on the brink of making a discovery, as he had said to Lapointe. Someone, Detective Chief Inspector Saint-Hubert, or the examining magistrate, had spoken to him and afterwards he had completely lost his thread.

The concierge had stated that a stranger had entered the building shortly after Doctor Fabre had left. He had given the Arescos' name, whereas the Arescos claimed they hadn't had any visitors and that no member of the family had gone out.

Maigret had had the residents questioned, but he'd neglected to go behind the scenes, to the servants' floor.

'Do you see, chief? . . . Wait! . . . There's more . . . That lock hadn't been forced either . . . So I went down to the third floor, via the backstairs, and I asked Madame Manu if she had the key to the maid's room . . . She reached up to a nail in the wall to the right of a shelf, and then stared at the wall and the nail in shock.

'"Goodness, it's gone . . ."'

'She told me she'd always seen the key to the sixth floor hanging from that nail.

'"Was it still there yesterday?" I pressed her.

'"I couldn't say for certain, but I'm almost positive . . . I've only ever been up once, with Madame, when I first came, to collect the sheets and blankets and stick paper around the windows to stop the dust getting in . . ."'

It was typical of Torrence who, once he was on the scent, followed it as tenaciously as a bloodhound.

'I went back upstairs, where my locksmith was waiting for me. The young Spanish woman, whose name is Dolores and whose hour off must have been up, had gone back downstairs.

'The lock is a basic, mass-produced model and my companion unlocked it easily.'

'You didn't ask Madame Josselin's permission?'

'No. I didn't see her. You told me not to disturb her unnecessarily. But we didn't need her. Well, chief, we're getting somewhere! Someone spent at least part of the night in the maid's room. The paper around the window was ripped, the window had been opened. It was still open when we went in. What's more, you can see that a man's lain on the mattress and rested his head on the bolster. And lastly, on the floor, there are cigarette ends. I say a man because there's no lipstick on the butts.

'I'm calling you from a bar called Le Clairon, in Rue Vavin. I thought you'd want to see this—'

'I'm on my way!'

Maigret was relieved not to have to think about Doctor Fabre any more. Everything had changed, or so it seemed. The concierge had not been mistaken. Someone had come in from the outside. That someone plainly knew not only about the revolver drawer but also about the existence of the maid's room and where the key hung in the kitchen.

So, the previous night, while the investigation was stalling on the third floor, the murderer had probably been in the building, lying on a mattress and smoking cigarettes as he waited for daybreak and the coast to be clear.

Since then, had there been a police officer on duty outside the front door at all times? Maigret didn't know. That was the job of the neighbourhood superintendent. There had been one when he'd come back from Rue du Saint-Gothard, but it was the concierge's husband who had requested it after the building had been besieged by reporters and photographers.

In any case, in the morning, there were bound to be a number of comings and goings, even if they were only deliveries. The concierge had been busy with the post, her baby and the reporters, some of whom had managed to sneak up to the third floor.

Maigret called Criminal Records.

'Moers? Would you send me one of your men with his fingerprinting kit? There might be some additional clues. Tell him to bring all his equipment . . . I'll be waiting for him in my office, yes . . .'

Inspector Baron knocked on his door.

'I finally managed to get hold of the general secretary of the Madeleine theatre, chief. Two seats were indeed booked in Madame Josselin's name. And the two seats were occupied. He doesn't know by whom, but they were occupied all evening. There was almost a full house, and no one left the auditorium during the performance. Of course, there are the intervals.'

'How many?'

'Two. The first one only lasts for fifteen minutes and few people leave their seats. The second one's longer, a good half-hour, because there's a complicated scenery change.'

'What time does that happen?'

'At ten o'clock. I have the name of the couple who were sitting immediately behind 97 and 99. They're regulars who always book the same seats, Monsieur and Madame Demaillé, Rue de la Pompe, in Passy. Shall I question them?'

'You better had . . .'

He didn't want to leave anything to chance. The forensic expert from Criminal Records arrived, his equipment slung over his shoulder like a magazine photographer.

'Shall I take a car?'

Maigret nodded and followed him. They found Torrence propped up on his elbows in front of a beer, still with his locksmith, who seemed to find the whole business very amusing.

'I don't need you any more,' said Maigret. 'Thank you.'

'How will you get in without me? I locked the door. Your inspector told me to—'

'I didn't want to take any chances,' muttered Torrence.

Maigret ordered a beer too, and downed it almost in one.

'It would be best if the three of you waited for me here.'

He crossed the street, entered the lift, and rang the Josselins' bell. Madame Manu opened the door as she had that morning, without taking off the chain, recognized him straight away and let him in.

'Which of the ladies do you wish to see?'

'Madame Josselin. Unless she's resting.'

'No. The doctor came earlier and insisted she go back to bed but she refused. It's not her style to stay in bed during the daytime, unless she's very ill.'

'No one has been here?'

'Only Monsieur Jouane, who stayed just a few minutes. Then your inspector, the fat one, who asked me for the key for upstairs. I swear to you I didn't touch it. As a matter of fact, I've been wondering why that key was left on the nail, seeing as no one used the room any more.'

'No one's ever used it since you've been working for Madame Josselin?'

'What would they have used it for, since there aren't any other servants?'

'Madame Josselin could have had one of their friends to stay, an acquaintance, even if it was only for a night?'

'If they'd had a friend to stay, I imagine they'd have given them Madame Fabre's room. I'll go and tell Madame—'

'What is she doing?'

'I think they're making the list of people to send the announcement to.'

The women weren't in the drawing room. After keeping Maigret waiting for a good while, they appeared together, and he had the strange sense that perhaps they stayed glued to one another because each was suspicious of the other.

'Forgive me for troubling you again, ladies. I presume Madame Manu has informed you?'

They observed each other before opening their mouths in unison, but it was Madame Josselin who spoke.

'It never occurred to me to put that key away,' she said, 'and I'd almost forgotten about it. What does this mean? Who could have taken it? Why?'

Her gaze was even more fixed, even darker than that morning. Her hands betrayed her jitteriness.

'So as not to bother you,' explained Maigret, 'my inspector took it upon himself to open the door of the maid's room. Please don't be angry with him. Especially since, in so doing, he has probably given the investigation a new lead.'

He watched her, alert to her reactions, but she gave no indication of what was going on inside her.

'What do you need to know?'

'How long is it since you last went up to the sixth floor?'

'Several months. When Madame Manu started working for me, I took her upstairs because the previous maid had left the place in a mess and the room was indescribably filthy.'

'So that was around six months ago?'

'Yes.'

'You haven't been back up there since? Your husband neither, I suppose?'

'He never went up to the sixth floor in his life. What would he have done up there?'

'And what about you, madame?' he asked Madame Fabre.

'I haven't been up there for years. Not since Olga, who

78

was so nice to me. I'd sometimes go up and see her in her room. Do you remember, mother? That must be nearly eight years ago . . .'

'There was paper stuck around the windows, wasn't there?'

'Yes, to keep the dust out.'

'The paper had been ripped and we found the window open. Someone had been lying on the bed, a man, probably, who smoked quite a few cigarettes.'

'Are you sure it was last night?'

'Not yet. I have come to ask for your permission to go up with my men and examine the place thoroughly.'

'I don't think it's up to me to give you permission.'

'Naturally, if you wish to be present—'

She stopped him by shaking her head.

'Did your last maid have a lover?'

'Not to my knowledge. She was a hard-working girl. She got engaged and left us to get married.'

Maigret made for the door. Why did he have the feeling again that there was a certain wariness, or animosity, between the mother and the daughter?

Once outside, he would have liked to know how they behaved when they were alone together, what they were saying to each other. Madame Josselin had maintained her composure, but Maigret was still convinced that she'd had a shock.

And yet he could have sworn that this business with the maid's room was not as much of a surprise to her as it had been to him. As for Véronique, she had turned abruptly to her mother with a questioning look in her eye.

What had she wanted to say when she'd opened her mouth?

He joined the three men at Le Clairon and drank another beer before going with them to the backstairs of the building. The locksmith opened the door. They had difficulty getting rid of him because he kept trying to make himself useful so he could stay.

'How will you lock it again without me?'

'I'll seal the door.'

'You see, chief,' Torrence was saying, pointing to the bed, the still-open window and the half-dozen or so cigarette ends on the floor.

'What I'd like to know first of all is whether those cigarettes were smoked recently.'

'That's easy.'

The expert inspected a cigarette butt, sniffed it, delicately undid the paper and rubbed the tobacco between his fingers.

'The laboratory tests will be more conclusive, but already I can tell you that these cigarettes were smoked not long ago. Besides, you'll notice that there's still a faint smell of tobacco in the air even though the window's open.'

The man unpacked his apparatus, with the slow, painstaking gestures of those who work in forensics. For them, there weren't any dead, or rather, the dead had no identity, as if they had no family, no personality. A crime was merely a scientific puzzle. They dealt with precise things: marks, clues, prints, dust.

'It's lucky the room hasn't been cleaned for a long time.'

And, turning to Torrence:

'Did you move around the room a lot? Did you touch anything?'

'Nothing, except for one of the cigarette ends. The locksmith and I stayed by the door.'

'Good.'

'Will you drop in to my office to give me the results?' asked Maigret, unsure what to do with himself.

'What about me?' asked Torrence.

'Go back to headquarters.'

'May I wait for a few minutes to see if there are any fingerprints?'

'If you insist.'

Maigret lumbered down the stairs, tempted to ring the bell of the third-floor service entrance. His last conversation with the two women had left him with a vaguely unpleasant feeling. He had a sense that things hadn't gone to plan.

Nothing, in fact, was going normally. But can you speak of 'normal' when you are dealing with people in whose home a murder has suddenly been committed? Supposing the victim had been a man like Pardon, for instance . . . How would Madame Pardon, her daughter and her son-in-law have reacted?

He couldn't imagine them, even though he'd known the Pardons for years and they were the Maigrets' closest friends.

In the heat of the moment, would Madame Pardon too have been dazed, unable to speak, and not wanted to stay beside her husband's body for as long as possible?

He'd just told them that a man had taken the key to the

maid's room from the kitchen and hidden himself up there for hours, and that he'd probably still been there when the two women were left alone after the departure of the police in the middle of the night.

But Madame Josselin had shown no emotion. As for Véronique, she had immediately looked at her mother, who seemed be stopping her from speaking out.

One thing was certain: the murderer hadn't stolen anything. And seemingly no one, at the present stage of the investigation, stood to benefit from René Josselin's death.

Josselin's death changed nothing for Jouane and his partner. And how could Jouane, who had only been to Rue Notre-Dame-des-Champs half a dozen times, know where the automatic was kept, or the key in the kitchen, or be familiar with the allocation of the maids' rooms on the sixth floor?

It was likely that Fabre had never been up there. And Fabre would have had no reason to hide in the maid's room. In any case, he wasn't there but at the hospital, initially, and then upstairs in the third-floor apartment, where Maigret had interviewed him.

On reaching the ground floor, Maigret abruptly headed for the lift, went up to the first floor and rang the Arescos' bell. Music could be heard coming from inside, and voices, a hubbub. When the door opened, he glimpsed two children chasing each other and a fat woman in a housecoat who was trying to catch them.

'Are you Dolores?' he asked the girl standing before him, now wearing a light-blue uniform with a matching cap on her black hair.

She was smiling broadly. In this apartment, everyone

seemed to be laughing and smiling, living in joyful chaos all day long.

'Sí, señor . . .'

'Do you speak French?'

'Sí . . .'

The fat woman spoke to the maid in Spanish, while looking Maigret up and down.

'Does she not understand French?'

The girl shook her head and burst out laughing.

'Tell her that I'm from the police, like the inspector you saw upstairs, and that I'd like to ask you some questions.'

Dolores translated, speaking with extraordinary rapidity, and the voluptuous woman grabbed one of the children by the arm, dragged him into a room and closed the glass door. The music was still playing. The girl remained in the doorway without inviting Maigret in. Another door opened a fraction, revealing the face of a man with dark eyes, and then closed noiselessly.

'What time did you go upstairs to bed last night?'

'Half past ten maybe . . . I didn't look.'

'Were you alone?'

'Sí, señor . . .'

'Did you meet anyone on the stairs?'

'No one.'

'What time did you hear a noise in the next room?'

'At six o'clock this morning, when I got up.'

'Someone walking around?'

'Cómo?'

She didn't understand the question and he mimed walking, which set her off laughing again.

'*Si . . . Si . . .*'

'Did you see the man who was walking around? Did the door open at all?'

'Was it a man?'

'How many people sleep up on the sixth floor?'

It took her a while to understand each question. She seemed to be translating word for word before grasping the meaning.

She showed two fingers, saying:

'Only two . . . There's the maid of the people on the fourth floor . . .'

'The Meurats?'

'I don't know . . . The Meurats, are they on the left or the right?'

'The left.'

'Then no. It's the others . . . They left with guns . . . I saw them yesterday morning putting them in the car.'

'Did their maid leave with them?'

'No. But she didn't come home to sleep. She has a boyfriend.'

'So you were alone, last night, up on the sixth floor?'

That made her laugh. Everything made her laugh. She didn't realize that there had been only a partition between her and a man who was almost certainly a murderer.

'All alone . . . No boyfriend.'

'Thank you.'

There were faces, dark eyes, behind the curtain over the glass door and most likely, once Maigret had left, more laughter would erupt.

He stopped in front of the lodge. The concierge wasn't

there. He found himself face to face with a man in braces holding a baby in his arms, which he hastily put in its cradle as he introduced himself.

'Officer Bonnet . . . Come in, inspector . . . My wife has just popped out to buy a few things . . . I'm on night duty this week so she's making the most of it.'

'I wanted to tell her that she wasn't mistaken. It seems that someone did enter the building last night and didn't leave.'

'Has he been found? Where?'

'No, he hasn't, but we found evidence in one of the maids' rooms . . . He must have left this morning, while your wife was battling with the reporters.'

'Is it my wife's fault?'

'Not at all.'

If it weren't for the extended holidays that most of the residents enjoyed, there would be five or six maids on the sixth floor and one of them might have chanced upon the murderer.

Maigret was loath to cross the road and return to Le Clairon again. In the end, though, he decided to go in, and without thinking ordered:

'A beer.'

A few moments later, through the window, he saw Torrence come out. He'd had enough of watching his colleague from forensics working and had had the same idea as Maigret.

'You here, chief?'

'I questioned Dolores.'

'Did you get anything out of her? Did she have her clothes on, at least?'

Torrence was still feeling proud of himself, happy with his discovery. He didn't seem to understand why Maigret appeared more preoccupied, more weighed down, than he had been that morning.

'We've got a lead, haven't we? You know there are fingerprints all over the place up there? Our colleague's having a field day. And if the murderer's got a criminal record . . .'

'I'm almost certain he hasn't,' sighed Maigret, draining his glass.

And indeed, two hours later, the Criminal Records clerk confirmed that the fingerprints found at Rue Notre-Dame-des-Champs didn't match anyone on file for being in trouble with the law.

Meanwhile Lapointe had spent the afternoon showing the photograph of René Josselin to local traders, park keepers and bench regulars. Some recognized him, others didn't.

'We saw him go past every morning, always walking slowly . . .'

'He used to watch the children playing . . .'

'He'd put his newspapers down next to him then start reading them, sometimes smoking a cigar . . .'

'He looked like a good man . . .'

Of course!

5.

Had it rained much during the night? Maigret had no idea, but on waking he was very happy to find the pavements a blackish colour, still glistening in places and reflecting real clouds, not the fluffy little pink ones of recent days but heavy, dark-rimmed rainclouds.

He was keen for the summer and the holiday season to be over, for everyone to be back in their place. He'd frown each time his eye lighted on a young woman in the street still sporting the tight trousers worn on the beach, feet bare and tanned, nonchalantly treading the Paris cobblestones in sandals.

It was Saturday. On waking up, he had intended to pay another visit to Jouane, in Rue du Saint-Gothard, without knowing why exactly. He wanted to see them all again, not so much to ask them specific questions as to mingle with them and gain a better feel for René Josselin's milieu.

There must be something that was eluding him. It did indeed now seem that the murderer had come from the outside, which extended the field of possibilities. But by how much? The fact remained that the automatic had been taken from the drawer, the key from its nail in the kitchen, and the man had known which room on the sixth floor to go into.

All the same, Maigret walked to his office, as he often

did; today he did so deliberately, as if to give himself a break. The air was cooler. People looked less tanned and wore their habitual facial expressions.

He reached Quai des Orfèvres just in time for the morning briefing and, with a file under his arm, he joined the other departmental chiefs in the commissioner's office. They each brought the commissioner up to date with their latest cases. The head of the Vice Squad, for instance, suggested closing a nightclub about which he received complaints almost daily. Meanwhile Darrui, also from Vice, had organized a nocturnal raid on the Champs-Élysées and three or four ladies of easy virtue were waiting at police headquarters for their fate to be decided.

'What about you, Maigret?'

'Me, I'm bogged down in a case involving good people,' he muttered with a smile.

'No suspect?'

'Not yet. Nothing but fingerprints that don't match our records, in other words, the fingerprints of an honest man . . .'

There had been a new murder during the night, a real one, almost a massacre. Lucas, barely back from his holiday, was handling it. For the time being, he was still shut away in his office with the murderer, trying to make sense of his explanations.

It had happened among the Polish community, in a slum near Porte d'Italie. A labourer who spoke little French, a puny, sickly-looking man called Stefan and whose surname was unpronounceable, lived there with a woman and four young children, as far as Lucas could gather.

Lucas had seen the woman before she'd been taken to hospital, and he claimed she was a splendid creature.

She wasn't the wife of the Stefan who had been arrested but of one of his compatriots, a certain Majewski, who had been working as an agricultural labourer for three years on farms in northern France.

Two of the children, the eldest, were Majewski's. What had happened exactly between these individuals three years earlier was hard to fathom.

'He gave her to me,' Stefan repeated obstinately.

At one point, he'd stated:

'He sold her to me.'

Be that as it may, three years earlier, the puny Stefan had taken Majewski's place in the slum dwelling and in the beautiful woman's bed. Her real husband had left, of his own free will, so it seems. Two more children were born and they all lived in one room like Romanies in their caravan.

But Majewski had taken it into his head to come back and, while Stefan was at work, had simply reclaimed his former place.

What had the two men said to one another on Stefan's return? That was what Lucas was trying to establish, and it was all the more difficult since his customer spoke French as badly as the Spanish or South American maid Maigret had questioned the previous day.

Stefan had left. He'd prowled around the neighbourhood for nearly twenty-four hours, not sleeping but hanging around various bars. Somehow or other he'd got hold of a sharp meat cleaver. He claimed he hadn't stolen it and was adamant about that, as if for him that was a point of honour.

During the previous night, he had entered the bedroom where they all slept and killed the husband with four or five blows from the cleaver. Then he'd thrown himself on the woman, who was screaming, her breasts bare, and attacked her two or three times, but some neighbours came rushing in before he was able to finish her off.

He had allowed himself to be arrested without putting up any resistance. Maigret went into Lucas' office and sat in on his interrogation for a while. Lucas was at his type-writer, painstakingly tapping out the questions and the replies.

The man was seated on a chair, smoking a cigarette he'd just been given, and there was an empty coffee cup beside him. He'd been somewhat roughed up by the neighbours. His shirt collar was torn, his hair dishevelled and his face scratched.

He was listening to Lucas speak, his eyebrows knitted, making a huge effort to understand, then he appeared to be thinking, his head swaying from left to right and from right to left.

'He gave her to me . . .' he repeated at length, as if that explained everything. 'He had no right to take her back.'

It seemed perfectly natural to him to have killed his former friend. He would have killed the woman too if the neighbours hadn't stopped him in time. Would he have killed the children?

He didn't answer that question, perhaps because he himself didn't know. He hadn't thought of everything.

He had decided to kill Majewski and his wife. As for the rest . . .

Maigret went back to his office. He found a note informing him that the people from Rue de la Pompe who had been behind Madame Josselin and her daughter at the theatre remembered the two women very clearly. They hadn't budged from their seats during the first interval, only during the second, after which they'd sat down again, well before the curtain had gone up, and they hadn't left the auditorium during the performance.

'What shall I do today, chief?' Lapointe had just asked him.

'The same as yesterday afternoon.'

In other words, retrace the route René Josselin took each morning on his stroll and question people.

'He must have spoken with someone. Try again, at the same time as him . . . Do you have a second photograph? Give it to me.'

Maigret stuffed it in his pocket, on the off chance. Then he took a bus to Boulevard de Montparnasse and had to put out his pipe because it was a bus with no external platform.

He needed to stay in touch with Rue Notre-Dame-des-Champs. Some colleagues claimed that he insisted on doing everything himself, including tedious shadowing, as if he didn't trust his inspectors. They didn't understand that for him it was a necessity to get a sense of people's lives, to try and put himself in their shoes.

Had it not been impossible, he would have moved into the Josselins' apartment and sat down at the table with the two women, and perhaps gone home with Véronique to observe how she behaved with her husband and children.

He wanted to walk in the steps Josselin took on his morning constitutional each day, to see what he saw and rest on the same benches.

Once again it was the hour when the concierge was sterilizing the baby's bottles and she was wearing her white pinafore.

'They've just brought the body back,' she said, still overwhelmed.

'Is the daughter upstairs?'

'She arrived about half an hour ago. Her husband dropped her off.'

'Did he go up?'

'No. He seemed to be in a hurry.'

'Is there anyone else in the apartment?'

'People from the funeral directors. They've already taken all their equipment upstairs to set up the chapel of rest.'

'Was Madame Josselin on her own last night?'

'No. At around eight o'clock, her son-in-law came with a lady of a certain age who was carrying a small suitcase and she stayed up there when he left. I presume she's a nurse or a companion. Madame Manu arrived at seven o'clock this morning, as usual, and now she's out at the market.'

He couldn't remember whether he had already asked the question and, if he had, he repeated it, because it was bothering him.

'You haven't noticed anyone hanging around the

building as if they were waiting, especially these past few days?'

She shook her head.

'Madame Josselin never had any visitors when her husband was out?'

'Not during the six years I've been here.'.

'What about him? He was often on his own in the afternoons. No one went up to see him? Did he ever go out for a few minutes?'

'Not to my knowledge . . . I think it would have struck me if he had . . . Of course, when there's nothing unusual going on, you don't pay attention to these things . . . I didn't take any more notice of them than of the other residents, less even, because they never gave me any trouble.'

'Do you know which side of the street Monsieur Josselin walked back on, on his way home?'

'It depended. I saw him come back from the direction of the Luxembourg Gardens, but sometimes he made a detour via Boulevard Montparnasse and Rue Vavin . . . After all, he wasn't a robot, was he?'

'Always alone?'

'Always alone.'

'Has Doctor Larue been back?'

'He dropped in yesterday in the late afternoon and stayed up there for quite some time.'

Another person Maigret would like to have talked to. He felt he had something to learn from all of them. He didn't necessarily suspect them of lying but of hiding part of the truth, wittingly or unwittingly.

Especially Madame Josselin. At no point had she seemed

relaxed. She was visibly on her guard, trying to guess in advance the questions he was going to ask her and mentally preparing her answers.

'Thank you, Madame Bonnet. Is the baby well? Did he sleep through the night?'

'He only woke up once and went straight back to sleep. Funnily enough, on that night, he was very restless, as if he could sense that something was going on . . .'

It was ten thirty. Lapointe must have been busy stopping people in the Luxembourg Gardens and showing them the photograph. They looked at it closely and shook their heads solemnly.

Maigret decided to have a go himself, on Boulevard de Montparnasse and then perhaps Boulevard Saint-Michel. He started by going into the little bar where he'd drunk three beers the previous day.

And the waiter asked him, as if he were a regular:

'The usual?'

He said yes, without thinking, even though he didn't fancy a beer.

'Did you know Monsieur Josselin?'

'I didn't know his name. When I saw his photo in the newspaper, I remembered him. In the past, he had a dog, an old German shepherd crippled with rheumatism that used to walk at his heels, hanging its head . . . I'm talking about at least seven or eight years ago. I've been working here for fifteen years.'

'What became of the dog?'

'It must have died of old age. I think it was mainly the young lady's dog . . . I remember her too.'

'Have you ever seen Monsieur Josselin in the company of a man? Have you ever had the impression that someone was waiting for him when he came out of his building?'

'No . . . You see, I only knew him by sight . . . He never came in here . . . One morning when I happened to be on Boulevard Saint-Michel, I saw him coming out of the PMU bar . . . That took me aback . . . I'm in the habit of having a little flutter on the horses every Sunday, but it surprised me that a man like him bets on the races.'

'Did you only see him at the PMU that one time?'

'Yes . . . But I'm rarely out and about at that hour.'

'Thank you.'

Next door was a grocer's shop, which Maigret entered, photograph in hand.

'Do you know this man?'

'Of course! It's Monsieur Josselin.'

'Did he used to come here?'

'Not him. His wife. They've been buying their groceries from us for fifteen years.'

'Does she always do her shopping herself?'

'She came in and left her order, and we delivered it a little later . . . Sometimes it was the maid . . . In the past, occasionally it was their daughter.'

'Have you ever seen her in the company of a man?'

'Madame Josselin?'

His question caused consternation and even a reprimand.

'She's not the sort of woman to have assignations with men, especially in the neighbourhood.'

Too bad! He would carry on asking his question all the same. He went into a butcher's.

'Do you know . . .?'

The Josselins didn't shop there and he received a rather curt reply.

Another bar. He entered and, since he'd started with beer, he ordered another and took the photograph out of his pocket.

'I think he lives around here . . .'

How many people would he and Lapointe question like this, each on their own patch? And yet they could only count on a coincidence. It was true that coincidence had already played a part. Maigret now knew that René Josselin had a passion, harmless as it may have been, a compulsion, a habit: he bet on the horses.

Did he play for high stakes? Or was he content to place small bets, for fun? Did his wife know? Maigret would have sworn she didn't. It wasn't in keeping with the apartment in Rue Notre-Dame-des-Champs or with their characters as he perceived them.

So there was a little chink. Might there not be others?

'Excuse me, madame . . . Do you . . .?'

The photo, once again. A shake of the head. He tried again further on, going into another butcher's, the right one this time, where Madame Josselin and Madame Manu were regular customers.

'We'd see him go past, almost always at the same time . . .'

'Alone?'

'Except when he ran into his wife on his way back from his walk.'

'What about her? Was she always alone too?'

'Once she came with a little boy who was just toddling, her grandson . . .'

Maigret went into a brasserie on Boulevard de Montparnasse. It was the hour when the place was almost empty. The waiter was polishing the counter.

'A little glass of anything but not beer,' he ordered.

'An aperitif? A brandy?'

'A brandy.'

And just when he was least expecting it, he made a breakthrough.

'I know him, yes. I immediately thought of him when I saw his photo in the newspaper. Except he wasn't quite so fat of late.'

'Did he come in for a drink sometimes?'

'Not often . . . He came perhaps five or six times, always when there was hardly anyone here, which is why I noticed him.'

'At this hour?'

'More or less . . . or a little later.'

'Was he alone?'

'No. There was someone with him and, each time, they'd sit right at the back.'

'A woman?'

'A man.'

'What type of man?'

'Well dressed. Not that old. I'd say he was in his early forties.'

'Did they appear to be discussing something?'

'They kept their voices down, so I couldn't hear what they were saying.'

'When was the last time they were here?'

'Three or four days ago.'

Maigret hardly dared believe it.

'Are you sure this is the man?'

He showed the photograph again. The waiter looked at it more attentively.

'I'm telling you it is! Listen! He was even carrying some newspapers, three or four at least and, when he left, I ran after him to give them back to him because he'd left them on the banquette.'

'Would you be able to recognize the man who was with him?'

'Maybe. He was tall, with brown hair . . . He was wearing a pale-coloured suit, of a lightweight fabric, very well cut.'

'Did they appear to be quarrelling?'

'No. They were serious, but they weren't quarrelling.'

'What did they drink?'

'The fat one, Monsieur Josselin, had a small bottle of mineral water and the other one a whisky. He must be used to it, because he wanted a particular brand. I didn't have it, so he asked for a different one.'

'How long did they stay?'

'Twenty minutes, perhaps? Maybe a little longer?'

'Was that the only time you saw them together?'

'I'd swear that when Monsieur Josselin came before, several months ago, well before the holidays, he was with the same person . . . And I saw that man again, as a matter of fact.'

'When?'

'The same day . . . In the afternoon . . . Or maybe it was

the following day? . . . No, it wasn't! It was definitely the same day.'

'So, this week?'

'Definitely this week . . . Tuesday or Wednesday.'

'Did he come back alone?'

'He was on his own for quite a while, reading an evening paper . . . He ordered the same whisky as in the morning . . . Then a lady joined him.'

'Do you know her?'

'No.'

'A young woman?'

'Of a certain age. Neither young nor old. An elegant lady.'

'Did they appear to know one another?'

'Definitely . . . She seemed to be in a hurry . . . She sat down next to him and when I went over to take their order she signalled that she didn't want anything.'

'Did they stay long?'

'About ten minutes . . . They didn't leave together . . . The woman went out first . . . And the man had another drink before going.'

'Are you certain that it's the same man who was with Monsieur Josselin that morning?'

'Absolutely positive . . . and he drank the same whisky.'

'Did you get the impression that he drinks heavily?'

'He seems like a man who drinks but can hold his liquor . . . He wasn't tipsy at all, if that's what you mean, but he had bags under his eyes . . . You see . . .?'

'Is that the only time you saw the man and the woman together?'

'The only one I recall . . . At certain times, you pay less attention . . . There are other waiters who work here . . .'

Maigret paid for his drink and found himself back in the street, wondering what to do next. Although he was tempted to go straight to Rue Notre-Dame-des-Champs, he was reluctant to turn up when the body had only just been returned to the family and they were busy setting up the chapel of rest.

He decided instead to keep walking to the Closerie des Lilas brasserie, going in and out of shops and showing the photograph with less and less conviction.

He met the Josselins' greengrocer and the cobbler who mended their shoes, and went into the patisserie where they bought cakes.

Then, as he reached Boulevard Saint-Michel, he decided to take it to get to the main entrance of the Luxembourg Gardens, following Josselin's daily route in reverse. Opposite the gates was the kiosk where Josselin bought his newspapers.

He showed the photograph. Questions, the same as always. He was expecting to see young Lapointe, who was working in the other direction, appear from one moment to the next.

'That's him all right . . . I kept his newspapers and weeklies for him.'

'Was he always alone?'

The old woman thought for a minute.

'Once or twice, I think . . .'

Once, in any case, there had been someone standing beside Josselin, and she'd asked:

'And for you?'

And the man had replied:

'I'm with monsieur.'

He was tall with dark hair, as far as she could recall. When was it? In the spring, because the horse chestnut trees were in blossom.

'And you haven't seen him again recently?'

'I haven't noticed him.'

Maigret found Lapointe in the PMU bar.

'Did they tell you too?' asked Lapointe in surprise.

'What?'

'That he was in the habit of coming here.'

Lapointe had already questioned the owner. He didn't know Josselin's name, but he was positive.

'He came in two or three times a week and bet five thousand francs each time.'

No! He didn't look like a punter. He didn't walk in holding the racing papers. He didn't study the odds.

'These days there are quite a lot like him who don't know which stables a horse belongs to or what the word handicap means . . . They pick numbers as if it's a lottery, ask for a ticket ending in such-and-such a number . . .'

'Did he sometimes win?'

'Once or twice.'

Maigret and Lapointe walked through the Luxembourg Gardens together. Students absorbed in their books sat on the iron chairs, and couples with their arms around each other gazed vaguely at the children playing under the watchful eye of their mother or their maid.

'Do you think Josselin kept secrets from his wife?'

'I get that impression. I'll find out soon.'

'Are you going to question her? Shall I come with you?'

'I'd rather you were there, yes.'

The funeral directors' van was no longer parked outside. The two men took the lift up and rang the bell, and once again Madame Manu opened the door a crack, leaving the chain on.

'Oh! It's you . . .'

She showed them into the drawing room where nothing had changed. The dining-room door was open, and an elderly woman was sitting near the window, knitting. Probably the nurse or companion that Doctor Fabre had brought over.

'Madame Fabre has just gone back home. Shall I inform Madame Josselin that you're here?'

And, in a whisper, the cleaner added:

'Monsieur is here . . .'

She pointed to Véronique's former bedroom, then went to let her employer know of their presence. Madame Josselin wasn't in the chapel of rest, and she walked in dressed in dark colours as she had been the previous day, with a grey pearl necklace and earrings.

She still looked as if she hadn't cried. Her stare was just as fixed, her eyes just as fiery.

'I understand you wish to speak to me?'

She looked at Lapointe with curiosity.

'One of my inspectors . . .' muttered Maigret. 'I apologize for disturbing you again.'

She did not invite them to sit down, as if she expected

the visit to be brief. Nor did she ask any questions, but her eyes looked straight into Maigret's.

'You may find this question pointless, but I would like to ask you first of all if your husband was a player.'

She didn't demur. Maigret even had the feeling that she was relieved, in a way, and her lips relaxed a little as she said:

'He used to play chess, usually with our son-in-law, sometimes, quite rarely, with Doctor Larue . . .'

'He didn't speculate on the stock exchange?'

'Never! He hated speculation. It was suggested to him a few years ago that he should turn his business into a limited company so as to expand, and he refused indignantly.'

'Did he buy national lottery tickets?'

'I never saw any in the house.'

'And he didn't bet on the horses either?'

'I think we went to the races at Longchamp or Auteuil no more than ten times in all, just to see . . . Once, a long time ago, he took me to see the Prix de Diane, at Chantilly, but he didn't go near the betting windows.'

'Might he have bet at a PMU?'

'What's that?'

'They're cafés and bars in Paris and all over France that have a licensed betting counter.'

'My husband didn't frequent cafés . . .'

There was a note of contempt in her voice.

'I presume you don't either?'

Madame Josselin's gaze hardened and Maigret wondered whether she was going to become angry.

'Why are you asking me that?'

He was reluctant to press his questioning further, thinking it was better not to alert her at this stage. The silence was painful and was beginning to weigh heavily on the three of them. Out of discretion, the nurse or companion had got up and closed the dining-room door.

Behind another door there was a dead man, black drapes, probably candles burning and a sprig of boxwood steeped in holy water.

Maigret could not forget that the woman in front of him was the widow. She had been at the theatre with her daughter when her husband was murdered.

'May I ask you whether on Tuesday or Wednesday of this week, you might have gone into a café . . . A local café . . .?'

'My daughter and I went for a drink when we left the theatre. Véronique was very thirsty. We didn't stay there long.'

'Where was that?'

'Rue Royale.'

'I'm talking about Tuesday or Wednesday and a local brasserie.'

'I don't understand what you mean.'

Maigret was embarrassed at the role he was having to play. He had the impression, without being certain, that the shot had hit home, that it was taking all of Madame Josselin's self-control not to let her panic show.

It had only lasted a fraction of a second and she hadn't taken her eyes off him.

'Someone, for some reason, could have arranged to

meet you close to here, on Boulevard de Montparnasse, for example . . .'

'No one arranged to meet me.'

'May I ask you to give me a photograph of you?'

She almost said:

'What for?'

She refrained, and contented herself with murmuring:

'I suppose I have to do as you ask.'

It was as if hostilities had just begun. She left the room and went into her bedroom, leaving the door open, and she could be heard rummaging in a drawer which must have been full of papers.

When she returned, she was holding a passport photo that was four or five years old.

'Presumably this is good enough?'

Maigret slipped it into his wallet, taking his time, and saying as he did so:

'Your husband used to bet on the horses.'

'In that case, it was behind my back. Is that against the law?'

'It isn't against the law, madame, but if we want to have a chance of finding his killer, we need to know everything. Three days ago, I didn't know this household. I knew neither of your existence, nor that of your husband. I asked you to cooperate . . .'

'I have answered you.'

'I would have liked you to tell me more.'

Since this was war, he attacked.

'I didn't insist on seeing you on the night of the tragedy because Doctor Larue told me you were in a state of utter shock . . . Yesterday, I came—'

'I received you.'

'And what did you tell me?'

'Everything I could tell you.'

'That means?'

'What I knew.'

'Are you certain you told me everything? Are you certain that your daughter and your son-in-law aren't hiding anything from me?'

'Are you accusing us of lying?'

Her lips trembled slightly. She was probably making a remarkable effort to remain upright and dignified in front of Maigret, whose complexion had grown somewhat ruddier. Lapointe meanwhile was embarrassed and didn't know where to look.

'Perhaps not of lying but of leaving out certain things . . . For example, I know for a fact that your husband used to bet on the horses . . .'

'How is that useful to you?'

'If you knew nothing about it, if you had never suspected him of it, this tells me he was capable of keeping things secret from you. And, if he hid that . . .'

'Maybe he never thought to tell me about it.'

'That would be plausible if he had only played once or twice, on impulse, but he was a regular, and gambled several thousand francs a week . . .'

'What are you suggesting?'

'You gave me the impression, which you have maintained, that you knew everything about him, and that you, for your part, had no secrets from him . . .'

'I don't understand what that has to do with—'

'Let us suppose that on Tuesday or Wednesday morning, he met someone in a brasserie on Boulevard de Montparnasse . . .'

'Did someone see him there?'

'There is at least one witness, who is positive.'

'He may have run into an old friend or a former employee who invited him for a drink . . .'

'You told me he didn't frequent cafés.'

'I wouldn't say that on an occasion like that—'

'He didn't mention it to you?'

'No.'

'He didn't say to you, when he got home:

'"By the way, I bumped into so-and-so . . ." '

'I don't remember.'

'If he had done so, would you remember?'

'Probably.'

'And supposing you yourself had met a man whom you know well enough to sit in a café with for around ten minutes while he drank a whisky . . .'

Perspiration beaded his forehead and he toyed almost menacingly with his extinguished pipe.

'I still don't understand.'

'Forgive me for disturbing you . . . I expect I'll have to come back . . . In the meantime, please think hard . . . Someone killed your husband and is still at large . . . He may kill again.'

She was very pale but still did not bat an eyelid and began to walk towards the door. She merely took her leave with a curt nod, then closed the door behind them.

In the lift, Maigret mopped his brow with his handkerchief. He seemed to be avoiding Lapointe's gaze, as if he were afraid of seeing an accusation in it, and he stammered:

'I had to . . .'

6.

The two men stood on the pavement a few paces from the apartment building, as if unwilling to part. A fine, barely perceptible drizzle was falling and at the bottom end of the street, high-pitched bells had started ringing, to which others responded from another direction, and then another.

A stone's throw from Montparnasse and its cabarets, this neighbourhood close to the Luxembourg Gardens was not only a quiet, middle-class haven, but it was also home to several convents. Behind the Little Sisters of the Poor there was the Servants of Mary; in neighbouring Rue Vavin was the Sisters of Zion, and, at the other end of Rue Notre-Dame-des-Champs, the Augustinian Sisters.

Maigret seemed to be listening to the chiming of the bells. He inhaled the air moist with invisible droplets, then sighed and said to Lapointe:

'Drop in to Rue du Saint-Gothard, would you? It will only take you a few minutes by taxi. On a Saturday, the offices and factory will probably be locked up. If Jouane is like his old boss, there's a chance that he'll have come in to finish off some urgent task on his own. If not, you're bound to find a concierge or watchman. If need be, ask for Jouane's home telephone number and call him.

'I'd like you to bring me a framed photograph that I saw

in his office. Yesterday, while he was talking to me, I looked at it absently without thinking it might be useful to me. It's a group photo with René Josselin in the centre, flanked by Jouane and Goulet most likely, with other male and female employees in rows behind them, thirty or so people altogether.

'Not all the women factory workers are there, only the longest-serving employees or the most senior. I suppose the photo was taken at a birthday celebration or when Josselin retired.'

'Shall I see you back at the office?'

'No. Come and meet me at the brasserie on Boulevard de Montparnasse, where I was earlier.'

'Which one is it?'

'I think it's called the Brasserie Franco-Italienne. It's next to a shop that sells artists' materials.'

Maigret went off, his shoulders stooped, drawing on his pipe, which he'd just lit and which, for the first time that year, had the taste of autumn.

He felt a lingering embarrassment at his harshness towards Madame Josselin and realized that this wasn't over but was just the start. Most likely she wasn't the only person who was hiding something from him or lying to him. And it was his job to uncover the truth.

It was always painful for Maigret to back someone into a corner, and that was because of an incident in his childhood, during his first year at school in his village in the Allier.

That was when he'd told his first ever big lie. The school gave out textbooks that were used, and some of them were badly battered. But some pupils bought brand new textbooks, and he wanted one.

One of the books he'd been given was a catechism with a greenish cover, its pages already yellowing, while other better-off friends had bought new catechisms, in a new edition with an attractive pink binding.

'I've lost my catechism,' he'd told his father. 'I told the teacher and he gave me another one.'

But he hadn't lost it. He'd hidden it in the attic, because he hadn't dared destroy it.

He had difficulty getting to sleep that night. He felt guilty and was convinced that sooner or later he would be found out. The next day, he experienced no joy in using his new catechism.

He had suffered for three or four days until he went to see the teacher, clutching his book.

'I've found the old one,' he stammered, red-faced, his throat dry. 'My father told me to give this one back to you.'

He still remembered the look the teacher gave him, a look that was both penetrating and benevolent. He was certain the man had guessed the whole story and had understood.

'Are you glad you've found it?'

'Oh yes, sir.'

All his life, he had remained grateful to that teacher for not having made him own up to his lie and thus saving him from humiliation.

Madame Josselin was lying too, but she wasn't a child, she was a woman, a mother, and a widow. He had, as it were, forced her to lie. And others around her were probably lying too, for one reason or another.

He would have liked to help them, save them from the terrible ordeal of fighting the truth. He wanted to believe they were good people; in fact he was convinced that they were. Neither Madame Josselin, nor Véronique, nor Fabre had killed.

But all the same, each of them was hiding something that would most likely have enabled him to lay hands on the murderer.

He glanced at the buildings opposite, thinking that it might be necessary to question all the residents of the street, all those who might have witnessed a useful little detail from their window.

Josselin had met a man, either the day before or on the day of his death, the waiter wasn't entirely sure. Maigret would find out whether it was indeed Madame Josselin who had met that same man in the afternoon, in the quiet ambiance of a brasserie.

He arrived there a little later and the atmosphere had changed somewhat. People were drinking aperitifs and a row of tables had already been set with tablecloths and cutlery for lunch.

Maigret went and sat in the same place as earlier that morning. The waiter who'd served him approached him as if he were already a regular customer, and Maigret took the passport photo out of his pocket.

'Do you think this is the woman?'

The waiter put on his glasses and studied the little cardboard square.

'She's not wearing a hat here, but I'm almost certain it's the same woman.'

'Almost?'

'I am certain. Only, if I have to give evidence in court one day, with the judges and the lawyers asking me lots of questions . . .'

'I don't think you will have to testify.'

'It's definitely her, unless it's someone who looks very much like her . . . She was wearing a dark woollen dress, not quite black, with sort of little grey hairs in the wool, and a hat with white trimming.'

The description of the dress matched the one Madame Josselin had been wearing that morning.

'What would you like to drink?'

'A brandy with water . . . Where's the telephone?'

'At the back on the left, opposite the toilet . . . Ask the cashier for a token.'

Maigret shut himself in the booth and looked for Doctor Larue's number. He wasn't too sure of finding him at home. He had no specific reason for calling the doctor.

He was doing the groundwork, as with the photo from Rue du Saint-Gothard. He was trying to rule out various hypotheses, even the most far-fetched.

A man's voice answered.

'Is that you, doctor? Maigret here.'

'I've just got home, and it just so happens I was thinking of you.'

'Why?'

'I don't know. I was thinking about your investigation, about your profession . . . You're lucky to find me at home at this hour . . . On Saturdays I finish my round earlier than on other days because many of my patients are away.'

'Would you mind coming and having a drink with me at the Brasserie Franco-Italienne?'

'I know it . . . I'll be there right away . . . Do you have any news?'

'I'm not sure yet.'

Larue, short, plump, balding, did not match the waiter's description of Josselin's companion. Neither did Jouane, whose hair was redder and who did not look like a whisky drinker.

Even so, Maigret was determined to leave no stone unturned. A few minutes later, the doctor got out of his car and joined him, then, addressing the waiter, said, as if on familiar territory:

'How are you, Émile? How are those scars?'

'They've almost disappeared. A port, doctor?'

They knew one another. Larue explained that he'd treated Émile a few months earlier, when the waiter had scalded himself with the percolator.

'Another time, a good ten years ago, he sliced himself with a cleaver . . . And how's your investigation going, inspector?'

'I'm not getting much help,' replied Maigret bitterly.

'Are you talking about the family?'

'About Madame Josselin, in particular. I'd like to ask you a couple of questions about her. I already asked you a few the other evening. There are a number of things bothering me. If I understand correctly, you and your wife were pretty much the Josselins' only close friends . . .'

'That's not entirely correct . . . As I told you, I've been the Josselins' physician for a long time and I knew

Véronique when she was a baby . . . But in those days, they only called me out very occasionally.'

'When did you become a family friend?'

'Much later. Once, a few years ago, we were invited to dinner along with some other people, the Anselmes. I still remember them, they're famous chocolate-makers . . . You must have heard of Anselme chocolates . . . They also make sugared almonds for baptisms . . .'

'Did they seem close to the Josselins?'

'They were on fairly friendly terms . . . They're a slightly older couple . . . Josselin supplied Anselme with boxes for the chocolates and sugared almonds.'

'Are they in Paris at present?'

'I'd be very surprised. Old Anselme retired four or five years ago and bought a house in Monaco . . . They live there all year round.'

'I'd like you to try very hard to remember. Who else have you met at the Josselins?'

'More recently, I have spent the evening at Rue Notre-Dame-des-Champs with the Mornets, who have two daughters and are on a cruise to Bermuda at the moment . . . They're paper merchants . . . In short, the Josselins only socialized with a few important customers and suppliers.'

'You don't recall a man in his forties?'

'I can't think . . . no . . .'

'You know Madame Josselin well . . . What do you know about her?'

'She's a woman of a very nervous disposition. I confess I treat her with sedatives, even though she possesses tremendous self-control.'

'Did she love her husband?'

'I'm certain she did . . . She didn't have a very happy adolescence, as far as I gather . . . Her father, widowed at a young age, was a bitter man, excessively strict.'

'Did they live near Rue du Saint-Gothard?'

'A stone's throw, Rue Dareau . . . She met Josselin and they got married after being engaged for one year.'

'What became of the father?'

'He contracted a particularly painful cancer and committed suicide a few years after becoming ill.'

'What would you say if you were told that Madame Josselin had a lover?'

'I wouldn't believe it. You see, through my profession, I am party to the secrets of many families. The number of women, especially in certain circles – the ones the Josselins move in – the number of women, I was saying, who are unfaithful to their husbands is much lower than literature and the theatre would have us believe.'

'I'm not claiming that it is always out of virtue. Perhaps lack of opportunity, fear of gossip are factors.'

'She often goes out alone in the afternoons . . .'

'Like my wife, like most wives . . . That doesn't mean that they're going to meet a man in a hotel or a so-called bachelor pad . . . No, inspector . . . If you are seriously asking me the question, my answer is a categorical no . . . You're barking up the wrong tree.'

'What about Véronique?'

'I'm tempted to reply the same thing, but I'd rather refrain . . . It's unlikely . . . It's not entirely impossible . . . She may have had a few dalliances before getting married . . .

She studied at the Sorbonne . . . She met her husband in the Latin Quarter and she must have met other men before him . . . Might she be a little disappointed by the life he has to lead? . . . I wouldn't swear it . . . She thought she was marrying a man and she's married a doctor . . . Do you understand?'

'Yes . . .'

That didn't get Maigret any further, didn't lead anywhere. He was floundering, and he drank his brandy glumly.

'Someone killed René Josselin . . .' he sighed.

So far, that was the only certainty. And also, that a mystery man had met the cardboard manufacturer in secret, in this same brasserie, and later had met Madame Josselin here.

In other words, the husband and the wife were hiding something from one another. Something connected with one and the same person.

'I don't see who it can be . . . I'm sorry I can't be of any more assistance . . . Now it's time for me to go back to my wife and children.'

Besides, Lapointe had arrived, a flat package under his arm, and was looking around for Maigret.

'Was Jouane in his office?'

'No. He wasn't at home either. They're spending the weekend at a sister-in-law's in the country. I promised the watchman I'd bring the photo back today and he didn't object too much.'

Maigret called the waiter and unwrapped the frame.

'Do you recognize anyone?'

The waiter put his glasses on again and scanned the rows of faces.

'Monsieur Josselin, of course, in the middle . . . He's a bit fatter in the photo than the man who came in the other day, but that's definitely him . . .'

'What about the others? . . . The people on his right and on his left?'

Émile shook his head.

'No. I've never seen them . . . He's the only one I recognize.'

'What will you have?' Maigret asked Lapointe.

'Anything.'

He looked at the reddish dregs in the doctor's glass.

'Is that port? . . . The same for me, waiter.'

'And for you, inspector?'

'Nothing, thank you . . . I think we'll have a bite to eat here.'

He didn't feel like going home to Boulevard Richard-Lenoir for lunch. A little later they moved into the restaurant section.

'She won't say anything,' complained Maigret, who'd ordered a choucroute. 'Even if I summon her to Quai des Orfèvres and question her for hours she'll keep her mouth shut.'

He resented Madame Josselin and at the same time he pitied her. She had just lost her husband in tragic circumstances, her entire life had been turned upside-down, and overnight she had become a woman on her own in an apartment that was too big, but that didn't stop the police from questioning her relentlessly.

What secret was she determined to keep at all costs? Although everyone's entitled to privacy, when a tragedy occurs, society demands an explanation.

'What do you plan to do, chief?'

'I don't know . . . Find that man, of course . . . He's not a thief . . . If he was the person who went and murdered Josselin the other night, he must have, or believe he has, compelling reasons.

'The concierge knows nothing . . . In the six years she's been there, she's never noticed any suspicious-looking visitors . . . This possibly goes back further in the past . . .

'I can't remember where she said that the previous concierge – who's her aunt – went to live out her old age . . . I'd like you to ask her, then find that woman and question her.'

'Supposing she lives in the country, in the middle of nowhere?'

'It might be worth going there or asking the local police to speak to her . . . Unless in the meantime someone decides to talk.'

Lapointe left too, stepping out into the drizzle, the framed photograph under his arm, while Maigret took a taxi to Boulevard Brune. The Fabres' apartment building was just as he had imagined: a huge, flat, dreary edifice which, although only a few years old, already appeared shabby.

'Doctor Fabre? Fourth floor on the right . . . You'll see a copper name plate on the door . . . If you're here for Madame Fabre, she's just gone out.'

To her mother's, probably, to finish sending out the announcements.

He stood rigidly in the narrow lift, pressed an electric buzzer and the little maid who opened the door automatically looked to his side, glancing up and down as if she expected him to have a child with him.

'Who do you want to see?'

'Doctor Fabre.'

'He's holding his surgery.'

'Be so good as to give him my card. I won't detain him for long.'

'Come this way . . .'

She opened the door of a waiting room where there were half a dozen mothers with children of various ages, and all eyes fixed on him.

He sat down, almost intimidated. There were building blocks on the floor and picture books on a table. A woman was rocking her baby, who was almost purple from screaming, keeping her eyes glued to the consulting-room door. Maigret knew they were all wondering:

'Is he going to be asked in before us?'

And because of his presence, they stopped talking. The wait lasted nearly ten minutes and when the doctor finally opened the door to his consulting room, he turned to Maigret.

He wore thick glasses which emphasized the tiredness in his eyes.

'Come in . . . I'm sorry I can't give you much time . . . Is it not my wife you have come to see? . . . She's at her mother's.'

'I know.'

'Have a seat.'

There was a set of baby scales, a glass-fronted cabinet full of nickel-plated instruments, and a sort of padded table covered with a sheet and an oilcloth. There was a jumble of papers on the desk, and books were piled on the mantelpiece and on the floor in one corner.

'How can I help?'

'Forgive me for disturbing you in the middle of your surgery, but I didn't know where I could find you alone.'

Fabre frowned.

'Why alone?' he asked.

'To be honest, I don't know. I find myself in a disagreeable situation and I thought you might be able to help me . . . You regularly visit your parents-in-law's home, so you must know their friends . . .'

'They had very few.'

'Have you ever met a man in his forties, dark hair, a fairly good-looking fellow?'

'Who is he?'

He too seemed to be on the defensive.

'I don't know. I have reason to believe that your father-in-law and your mother-in-law both knew a man answering to this general description.'

The doctor stared vacantly through his lenses at a point in space. Maigret gave him time to think, and eventually grew impatient.

'Well?'

As if surfacing from a dream, Fabre asked him:

'What? What do you want to know?'

'Do you know him?'

'I don't see who you mean. Generally, when I went to

their home, it was in the evening to keep my father-in-law company while the women went to the theatre.'

'But all the same, you know their friends . . .'

'Some of them . . . Not necessarily all . . .'

'I thought they seldom entertained.'

'Very seldom, that's true . . .'

It was exasperating. He looked everywhere except in Maigret's direction and he seemed to be finding the conversation a painful ordeal.

'My wife used to see a lot more of her parents than I did . . . My mother-in-law came here almost daily . . . when I was either in my consulting room or at the hospital.'

'Did you know that Monsieur Josselin used to bet on the horses?'

'No. I thought he rarely went out in the afternoons.'

'He played at the local PMU.'

'Oh!'

'His wife didn't know either, apparently. So, he didn't tell her everything.'

'Why would he have told me about it? I was only his son-in-law.'

'Madame Josselin, meanwhile, kept certain things secret from her husband.'

He did not protest. He seemed to be saying to himself, like at the dentist's: A few more minutes and it'll be over . . .

'One afternoon this week, Tuesday or Wednesday, she met a man in a brasserie on Boulevard de Montparnasse—'

'That's none of my business, is it?'

'You're not surprised?'

'I assume she had her reasons for meeting him.'

'Monsieur Josselin had met the same man in the same brasserie that morning, and seemed to know him well . . . That doesn't mean anything to you?'

The doctor took some time before shaking his head, looking perturbed.

'Now listen to me, Monsieur Fabre. I understand that you are in a delicate situation. Like any man who gets married, from that moment on you became part of a family that you didn't know before.

'That family inevitably has its little secrets. It is highly unlikely that you wouldn't have discovered some of them. It is of no importance so long as no crime is committed. But your father-in-law has been murdered and you were very nearly the main suspect.'

He did not object, did not react at all. There could have been a glass partition between them which prevented words from being heard.

'This isn't a financially motivated crime. It was no burglar caught red-handed who killed Monsieur Josselin. He knew the apartment as well as you did, the household's routines, the place of each object. He knew that your wife and her mother were at the theatre that evening and that you would probably be spending the evening with your father-in-law.

'He knew where you live, and it is most likely he who telephoned here so that the maid would call you, and who sent you to Rue Julie . . . Do you agree?'

'It sounds plausible . . .'

'You said yourself that the Josselins entertained seldom and had no close friends so to speak.'

'I see.'

'Could you swear to me that you have no idea who this man could be?'

The doctor's ears had turned red and his face looked more exhausted than ever.

'I'm sorry, inspector, but there are children waiting.'

'You refuse to speak?'

'If I had any specific information to give you . . .'

'You mean you have suspicions, but they aren't precise enough?'

'Take it as you wish . . . May I remind you that my mother-in-law has just suffered a terrible shock and that she's a very highly-strung person, even if she doesn't show her emotions.'

He stood up and went over to the door that opened into the passage.

'Don't hold it against me . . .'

He did not proffer his hand but simply nodded goodbye. The little maid appeared as if by magic and showed Maigret out of the apartment.

He was furious, not only with the young paediatrician but with himself, because he had the feeling that he'd gone about things the wrong way. Fabre was probably the only member of the family who could have talked, but Maigret had got nothing out of him.

No! There was one thing: Fabre hadn't registered any surprise when Maigret had mentioned his mother-in-law's meeting with the stranger in the brasserie. It hadn't shocked him. Nor had it surprised him to learn that Josselin had met the same man, in secret, in the gloom of the same brasserie.

He envied Lucas, who had already finished with his Polish killer and was probably quietly writing his report.

Maigret walked on the pavement, watching out for a taxi, but they all had their flags down. The drizzle had turned into proper rain and once more the streets were full of glistening umbrellas.

'If the man met René Josselin and his wife one after the other . . .'

He tried to reason, but he lacked the foundations. Had the stranger also contacted the daughter, Madame Fabre? And why not Fabre himself?

And why was the entire family protecting him?

'Hey! . . . Taxi! . . .'

At last he found one that was free, and hurriedly got in.

'Keep driving . . .'

He didn't know where he was going yet. His initial instinct had been to ask to be taken to Quai des Orfèvres, to get back to his office and shut himself in so he could grumble to his heart's content. Had Lapointe perhaps discovered something new? He had the feeling, without being certain, that the former concierge had moved away from Paris and was somewhere in Charente or central France.

The driver went slowly, turning around from time to time with an inquiring look.

'What shall I do at the traffic lights?'

'Turn left.'

'As you wish . . .'

And suddenly Maigret leaned forward.

'Drop me in Rue Dareau.'

'Whereabouts in Rue Dareau? It's a long street.'

'On the corner of Rue du Saint-Gothard.'

'Very well.'

Maigret was exhausting all the possibilities, one after the other. He had to take his notebook out of his pocket to remind himself of Madame Josselin's maiden name: de Lancieux . . . and he remembered that the father had been a retired colonel.

'Excuse me, madame . . . How long have you been the concierge in this building?'

'Eighteen years, my good sir, which dates me a bit.'

'Did you ever know a former colonel and his daughter who lived around here and whose name was de Lancieux?'

'Never heard of them . . .'

Two, three apartment buildings. The first concierge, even though middle-aged, was too young. The second didn't remember and the third wasn't more than thirty years old.

'You don't know what number?'

'No. I only know that it was near Rue du Saint-Gothard.'

'You could ask opposite . . . The concierge is at least seventy . . . Speak up, because she's a bit hard of hearing.'

He almost shouted. She shook her head.

'I don't remember a colonel, no, but my memory's gone . . . Since my husband was run over by a lorry, I haven't been the same . . .'

He was leaving to try elsewhere. She called him back.

'Why don't you ask Mademoiselle Jeanne?'

'Who's that?'

'She's lived here for at least forty years . . . She doesn't come down because of her legs . . . It's on the sixth floor, at the end of the corridor . . . The door's never locked . . . Knock and go in . . . You'll find her in her armchair by the window.'

And he did find her, a wizened little old woman, but her cheeks were still rosy and she had a childlike smile.

'Lancieux? . . . A colonel? . . . Yes, of course I remember them . . . They used to live on the second floor, on the left . . . They had an old servant who was very grumpy and fell out with all the shopkeepers. In the end she had to do her shopping in another neighbourhood.'

'The colonel had a daughter, didn't he?'

'A dark-haired girl, who wasn't in good health. Nor was her brother, poor thing. They had to send him to the mountains because he was consumptive.'

'Are you certain she had a brother?'

'As sure as I can see you. And I can see you very clearly, despite my age. Why won't you sit down?'

'You don't know what became of him?'

'Who? The colonel? He put a bullet through his brain, and the whole place was topsy-turvy. It was the first time something like that had happened around here . . . He was ill too, cancer apparently . . . But even so, I don't approve of him killing himself.'

'What about his son?'

'What?'

'What became of him?'

'I don't know . . . The last time I saw him was at the funeral.'

'Was he younger than his sister?'

'About ten years.'

'You've never heard any news of him?'

'You know, in buildings like this, people come and go . . . If I were to count all the families who have lived in their apartment since . . . Is it the young man you're interested in?'

'He's no longer a young man . . .'

'If he's cured, he definitely isn't . . . He's probably married with children too.'

She added, her eyes twinkling mischievously:

'Me, I never married and that's probably why I'll live to be a hundred . . . You don't believe me? . . . Come back and see me in fifteen years . . . I promise you I'll still be in this armchair . . . What do you do for a living?'

Maigret thought it unwise to risk giving her a shock by saying he was from the police so he merely replied, as he looked for his hat:

'Research.'

'Well, no one can say that you don't dig deep into the past . . . I doubt there's anyone left in the street who remembers the Lancieux . . . It's for an inheritance, isn't it? The heir's lucky that you came across me . . . You can tell him . . . He might be generous enough to send me some sweets.'

Half an hour later, Maigret was sitting in the office of examining magistrate Gossard. He looked relaxed and a little gloomy as he told his story in a calm, monotonous voice.

The magistrate listened solemnly and, when Maigret had finished, there was a fairly long silence during which they could hear the water gurgling in one of the gutters of the Palais de Justice.

'What do you intend to do?'

'To summon them all this evening to Quai des Orfèvres. It will be easier and above all less painful than at Rue Notre-Dame-des-Champs.'

'Do you think they'll talk?'

'One of the three is bound to talk eventually.'

'Do as you see fit.'

'Thank you.'

'I wouldn't like to be in your shoes . . . Go easy on her all the same . . . Don't forget that her husband—'

'I haven't forgotten, believe me. That's why I'd rather see them in my office . . .'

A quarter of Parisians were still on holiday by the sea or in the country. Others had started hunting while others still were on the roads, looking for a quiet spot for the weekend.

Meanwhile Maigret walked slowly down the long, empty corridors, on his way down to his office.

7.

It was 5.55 p.m. Again, because it was Saturday, most of the offices were empty and there was no activity in the vast corridor where, at the very end, a lone man sat brooding outside the door to an office, wondering whether he'd been forgotten. The commissioner had just left, after going in to shake Maigret's hand.

'Are you going to give it a try this evening?'

'The sooner the better. Tomorrow, family may be arriving from the country, because those people probably have a lot of close and distant relatives. Monday's the funeral so in all decency I can't choose that day . . .'

For the past hour, Maigret had been occasionally pacing up and down his office, his hands behind his back, smoking one pipe after another, preparing what he hoped would be the showdown. He didn't like the word 'staging'. He called this 'prepping' as in a restaurant kitchen, and he was always anxious not to forget the slightest detail.

At five thirty, having issued all his instructions, he went down to the Brasserie Dauphine for a large beer. It was still raining. The air was grey. He ended up drinking two beers in quick succession, as if he were expecting it to be a long while before he'd have the chance for another one.

Back in his office, all he needed to do was wait. Eventually there was a knock at the door and it was Torrence who arrived first, looking eager and self-important, his face animated, as it always was when he was entrusted with a sensitive mission. He carefully shut the door behind him, and made it sound as if he'd pulled off a huge feat when he announced:

'The women are here!'

'In the waiting room?'

'Yes. They're alone. They seemed surprised that you didn't receive them straight away, especially the mother. I think she's annoyed.'

'How did it go?'

'When I arrived at their place, the cleaning lady opened the door. I told her who I was, and she grunted:

'"Again!"

'The door to the drawing room was closed. I had to wait quite some time and I could hear whispering, but I couldn't make out what was being said.

'Finally, after a good fifteen minutes, the door opened and I glimpsed a priest being shown out of the front door. It was the mother who was with him.

'She looked at me as if she was trying to place me, then she invited me to follow her. The daughter was in the drawing room and her eyes were red, as if she'd been crying.'

'What did the mother say on seeing the summons?'

'She re-read it twice. Her hand was trembling slightly. She gave it to her daughter, who also read it then looked at her as if to say:

'"I knew it. I warned you . . ."

'It all happened as if in slow motion and I felt very uncomfortable.

'"Do we have to go there?"

'I said yes. The mother added:

'"With you?"

'"Well, I've got a car downstairs. But if you'd rather take a taxi . . ."

'They whispered together and seemed to come to a decision, then they asked me to wait a few minutes.

'I was left alone in the drawing room for ages while they got themselves ready. They called an old woman who was in the dining room, and she followed them into one of the bedrooms.

'When they came back, they had their hats and coats on, and they were putting on their gloves.

'The cleaning woman asked if she should wait for them for dinner. Madame Josselin replied grudgingly that she had no idea . . .

'They settled themselves in the back of the car and didn't open their mouths once during the journey. I could see the daughter in the rear-view mirror and she seemed to be the more anxious one. What do you want me to do?'

'Nothing for now. Wait for me in the office.'

Then it was the turn of Émile, the waiter, who looked a lot older in a jacket and raincoat.

'I'm going to ask you to wait in another room.'

'It won't be too long, will it, inspector? Saturday nights are busy, and the other waiters will be annoyed with me if I leave them to do all the work . . .'

'Once I call you, it will only take a few minutes.'

'And I won't have to testify in court? Promise?'

'I promise.'

An hour earlier, Maigret had telephoned Doctor Fabre, who had listened in silence, then said:

'I'll do my utmost to be there at six o'clock. It depends on my consultation.'

He arrived at five past six and must have seen his wife and mother-in-law through the windows of the waiting room as he walked past. Maigret went to have a look, from a distance, at the room, with its green chairs and its three walls covered in framed photographs of police officers killed in the line of duty.

The electric light was on all day. The atmosphere was bleak, depressing. He remembered certain suspects who had been left there to mope for hours, as if they had been forgotten, to wear down their resistance.

Madame Josselin sat ramrod straight, absolutely still, while her daughter kept standing up and sitting down again.

'Come in, Monsieur Fabre.'

Because of the summons, the doctor was expecting a new development in the case and looked worried.

'I came as quickly as I could,' he said.

He had no hat, coat or raincoat. He must have left his doctor's bag in his car.

'Have a seat . . . I shan't detain you for long.'

Maigret sat down at his desk facing him, took the time to light his pipe, which he'd just filled, and said softly, with a hint of reproach in his voice:

'Why didn't you tell me that your wife had an uncle?'

Fabre must have been anticipating the question, but his ears still turned beetroot, as they did at the slightest emotion.

'You didn't ask me,' he replied, trying to sustain Maigret's gaze.

'I asked you to tell me who was a regular visitor to your parents-in-law's apartment.'

'He wasn't a regular visitor.'

'Does that mean that you have never seen him?'

'Yes.'

'He didn't attend your wedding?'

'No. I was aware of his existence because my wife had told me about him, but no one at Rue Notre-Dame-des-Champs ever talked of him, at least not in front of me.'

'Be honest, Monsieur Fabre . . . When you found out that your father-in-law was dead, that he'd been murdered, when you found out that he'd been shot with his own revolver and that the culprit must therefore be someone who was familiar with the apartment, did you immediately think of him?'

'Not straight away . . .'

'What made you think of him?'

'My mother-in-law and my wife's attitude.'

'Did your wife talk to you about him when you were alone together?'

He thought for a moment.

'We have hardly been alone together since it happened.'

'And she didn't say anything to you?'

'She told me she was afraid.'

'Of what?'

'She didn't say . . . She was thinking mostly of her mother . . . I am only a son-in-law . . . They welcomed me into the family, but I am not entirely part of it . . . My father-in-law was very generous towards me . . . Madame Josselin adores my children . . . But all the same, there are some things that are none of my business . . .'

'Are you saying your wife's uncle hasn't set foot in the apartment during the time you've been married?'

'All I know is that there was a quarrel, that they felt sorry for him but could no longer have him in their home, but I didn't probe into the reasons why . . . My wife spoke of him as a poor soul more to be pitied than blamed, sort of half-mad.'

'Is that all you know?'

'That's all. Are you going to question Madame Josselin?'

'I have no option.'

'Don't be too tough with her. She appears to be in control of herself. Some people misinterpret that and take her for a hard woman. But I know that actually she's hyper-sensitive but is incapable of expressing her emotions. Since her husband's death, I've been expecting her nerves to crack at any moment.'

'I'll treat her as gently as possible.'

'Thank you . . . Is that all?'

'You can go back to your patients now.'

'May I have a word with my wife on the way out?'

'I'd rather you didn't speak to her and above all not to your mother-in-law.'

'In that case, tell her that if I'm not at home when she gets back, I'll be at the hospital . . . I received a phone call as I was leaving and it's likely I'll have to operate.'

As he reached the door, he changed his mind and retraced his steps.

'I apologize for being so rude to you earlier . . . Consider my situation . . . I have been generously welcomed into a family that is not mine . . . This family has its problems, like any other . . . I felt it wasn't my place to—'

'I understand, Monsieur Fabre.'

He too was a good man, of course! Better than a good man, probably, according to everyone who knew him. This time, the two men shook hands.

Maigret opened the door to the inspectors' office and showed Émile into his own office.

'What do you want me to do?'

'Nothing. Stay over there, by the window. I might ask you a question and you can answer.'

'Even if it's not the answer you're hoping for?'

'Just tell the truth.'

Maigret went to fetch Madame Josselin, who rose to her feet at the same time as her daughter.

'Please follow me . . . Only you . . . I'll speak with Madame Fabre later.'

She was wearing a black dress with a grey heather effect, a black hat trimmed with little white feathers and a light camel-hair coat. Maigret had her precede him and she immediately saw the man standing by the window, wringing his hat in embarrassment. She seemed surprised, turned to Maigret and, since no one said anything, she eventually asked:

'Who is this?'

'Don't you recognize him?'

She studied him more closely and shook her head.

'No.'

'What about you, Émile, do you recognize this lady?'

In a voice husky with emotion, the waiter replied:

'Yes, inspector. It's definitely her.'

'Is she the lady who came to the Brasserie Franco-Italienne one afternoon at the beginning of the week to meet a man of around forty? Are you certain?'

'She was wearing the same dress and the same hat . . . I described them to you this morning.'

'Thank you, you may go.'

Émile darted a look at Madame Josselin that seemed to be apologizing for what he had just done.

'You won't need me any longer?'

'I don't think so.'

The two of them remained alone, and Maigret indicated an armchair facing his desk. He took his place behind the desk but did not sit down straight away.

'Do you know where your brother is?' he asked softly.

She looked straight at him, her eyes dark and shining, as she had done at Rue Notre-Dame-des-Champs, but she was less tense and seemed almost to exude a sense of relief. This was even more pronounced when she decided to sit down. It was as if she'd finally made up her mind to abandon the façade she'd been desperately battling to maintain.

'What did my son-in-law tell you?' she asked, answering one question with another.

'Very little . . . He merely confirmed that you had a brother, which I already knew.'

'Who told you?'

'A very elderly lady almost in her nineties whose home is still in Rue Dareau, in the building where you used to live with your father and your brother.'

'It was bound to happen . . .' she murmured.

He pursued his line of attack:

'Do you know where he is?'

She shook her head.

'No. And I swear I'm telling the truth. Until Wednesday I was even convinced that he was a long way from Paris.'

'He never wrote to you?'

'Not since he no longer set foot in our apartment.'

'Did you know straight away that he was the person who had killed your husband?'

'I'm still not absolutely sure it was him . . . I refuse to believe it . . . I know that everything points to him . . .'

'Why were you trying to protect him at all costs, by saying nothing and forcing your daughter to say nothing?'

'First of all because he's my brother and because he's a poor soul . . . And secondly because I feel partly to blame . . .'

She took a handkerchief out of her handbag but not to wipe her eyes, which were dry and still burning with an inner fever. Mechanically, her thin fingers rolled it into a ball while she spoke or waited for Maigret's questions.

'Now I'm ready to tell you everything.'

'What is your brother's name?'

'Philippe . . . Philippe de Lancieux . . . He's eight years younger than me.'

'As I understand it, he spent part of his adolescence in a mountain sanatorium?'

'Not his adolescence . . . He was only five when he was diagnosed with tuberculosis . . . The doctors sent him to Haute-Savoie where he stayed until he was twelve.'

'Was your mother already dead?'

'She died a few days after he was born . . . and that explains a lot . . . I suppose everything I'm about to tell you will be splashed all over the newspapers tomorrow . . .'

'I promise you that won't happen. What does your mother's death explain?'

'My father's attitude towards Philippe and in fact his attitude in general during the second half of his life . . . From the day my mother died, he became a different man and I am convinced he couldn't help resenting Philippe, blaming him for his wife's death.

'What's more, he started drinking . . . It was around that time he left the army, even though he had no fortune to speak of, so we lived very frugally.'

'While your brother was in the mountains, did you stay in Rue Dareau alone with your father?'

'An old servant, who's dead now, lived with us until the end.'

'And on Philippe's return?'

'My father put him in a religious education establishment in Montmorency and we barely saw my brother except during the holidays . . . At fourteen, he ran away and, two days later, he was found in Le Havre, having hitch-hiked there.

'He told people he had to get to Le Havre as quickly as possibly because his mother was dying . . . He was already in the habit of making things up . . . He would invent some story and people believed him, because he ended up believing it himself.

'The school in Montmorency wouldn't take him back, so my father sent him to a new one, near Versailles.

'He was still there when I met René Josselin . . . I was twenty-two . . .'

The handkerchief had now been twisted into a rope which she tugged at with her clenched hands, and Maigret had unwittingly let his pipe go out.

'That was when I made a mistake and I've always been angry at myself . . . I was only thinking of myself.'

'Did you have second thoughts about getting married?'

She looked at him, uncertain, trying to find the right words.

'This is the first time I'm having to speak about these things, which I've always kept to myself . . . Life with my father had become all the more difficult since, unbeknown to us, he was already ill . . . And I realized that he wouldn't live to a ripe old age and that, one day, Philippe would need me . . . You see, I shouldn't have married . . . I said so to René.'

'Were you working?'

'My father wouldn't allow it, because he believed a young woman's place was not in an office . . . All the same, I planned to get a job and live with my brother later . . . René was insistent . . . He was thirty-five . . . He was in the prime of life and I trusted him completely.

'He told me that, whatever happened, he would take care of Philippe and treat him like his own son, and I eventually gave in.

'I shouldn't have . . . That was the easy option . . . Overnight, I escaped from the oppressive atmosphere at home and I shrugged off my responsibilities.

'I had a feeling—'

'Did you love your husband?'

She looked him straight in the eyes and said with a sort of defiance in her voice:

'Yes, inspector . . . and I loved him to the end . . . He was the man—'

For the first time, her voice faltered, and she turned away for a moment.

'But all the same, I have always thought I should have been more selfless . . . When, two months after we were married, the doctor told me that my father had an incurable cancer, it seemed like a punishment.'

'Did you say so to your husband?'

'No. Everything that I'm telling you today, I'm saying for the first time, because if my brother really did what you think he did, it's the only thing I can offer in his defence . . . If necessary, I'll repeat it in the witness box . . . Contrary to what you might think, I don't care what people say.'

She was animated now, and her hands were increasingly busy. She opened her handbag again and took out a small metal box.

'Would you give me a glass of water? . . . I'd better take one of these pills that Doctor Larue prescribed.'

Maigret went over and opened the cupboard in which there was a wash-basin, a glass and even a bottle of brandy, which sometimes came in useful.

'Thank you . . . I'm trying to stay calm . . . People have always thought that I have great self-control, but they have no idea what it costs me to keep up the pretence . . . What was I saying?'

'You were talking about your marriage . . . Your brother was at school in Versailles at the time . . . Your father . . .'

'Yes . . . My brother only stayed at Versailles for one year before he was thrown out.'

'Did he run away again?'

'No, but he was wild, and his teachers couldn't get anywhere with him . . . You see, I never lived with him long enough to really get to know him . . . I'm sure that, deep down, he's not a bad person . . . It's his imagination that plays tricks on him . . .

'Perhaps it's a result of spending his childhood in a sanatorium, lying in bed most of the time, cut off from the world.

'I remember an answer he gave me, one day, when I found him lying on the floor in the attic, after we'd been looking all over for him.

'"What are you doing, Philippe?"

'"I'm telling myself stories . . ."

'Unfortunately, he told other people stories too. I suggested to my father that he come and live with us. René agreed. It was even his idea in the first place. My father didn't want him to, and sent him to another boarding school, in Paris this time.'

'Philippe used to come and visit us every week in Rue Notre-Dame-des-Champs, where we were already living . . . My husband really did treat him like his own son . . . But then, Véronique was born . . .'

A quiet, peaceful street, a comfortable apartment surrounded by convents, a stone's throw from the leafy Luxembourg Gardens. Good people. A prosperous business. A happy family . . .

'Then you know what happened to my father . . .'

'Where did it occur?'

'Rue Dareau. In his armchair. He put on his uniform and placed portraits of my mother and of me in front of him. Not of Philippe . . .'

'What became of him?'

'He carried on with his studies as best he could. He lived with us for two years. It was clear that he'd never take his baccalaureate and René intended to give him a job in his company.'

'How well did your brother and your husband get along?'

'René had endless patience . . . He kept my brother's escapades from me as far as possible and Philippe took advantage . . . He couldn't cope with any boundaries, any discipline . . . He often didn't turn up for meals and he'd come home at all hours, always with an extraordinary tale to tell.

'The war broke out . . . Philippe was expelled from one last school and my husband and I were increasingly concerned about him, although we said nothing to one another.

'I think that René too had regrets . . . Maybe if I'd stayed at Rue Dareau . . .'

'I don't agree,' said Maigret, solemnly. 'You can be certain that your marriage made no difference to the course things took.'

'Do you think so?'

'During my career I've seen dozens like your brother, who didn't have the same excuses as he did.'

She desperately wanted to believe him, but couldn't quite bring herself to do so yet.

'What happened during the war?'

'Philippe was determined to enlist . . . He had just turned eighteen and he was so insistent that we eventually gave in.

'In May 1940, he was taken prisoner in the Ardennes and we had no news from him for a very long time.

'He spent the entire war in Germany, first of all in a camp, then on a farm in the Munich area.

'We hoped he'd come back a different man . . .'

'But he hadn't changed?'

'Physically, he was definitely a man, and I barely recognized him. The outdoor life had done him good and he had become robust, vigorous. From the first tales he told we realized that, deep down, he was still the boy who kept running away and who told himself stories.

'To listen to him, he'd had the most extraordinary adventures. He'd escaped three or four times, in incredible circumstances.

'He'd lived as man and wife with the farm woman for whom he worked, which is plausible, and he claimed she'd

144

had two children by him . . . She had another by her husband.

'This husband, according to Philippe, had been killed at the Russian front . . . My brother talked of going back there, marrying the farm woman and staying in Germany . . .

'Then, a month later, he had other plans . . . He was tempted to go to America and he said he'd met some secret service agents who would be only too happy to welcome him.'

'Did he work?'

'My husband found him a job at Rue du Saint-Gothard, as promised.'

'Did he live with you?'

'He only stayed with us for three weeks before moving in with a waitress near Saint-Germain-des-Prés . . . Again, he talked of getting married. Each time he had a new affair, he made wedding plans.

'"She's expecting a baby, you see, and if I didn't marry her, I'd be a bastard."

'I've given up counting the number of children he claims to have had all over the place.'

'Was he lying?'

'My husband tried to find out. He never managed to obtain convincing proof. Each time, it was a means of getting money out of him.'

'And I soon discovered my brother was hedging his bets. He came and confided in me, and begged me to help him. He always needed a certain amount of money to get himself out of a mess, after which everything would be fine.'

'Did you give him what he asked for?'

'I nearly always gave in. He knew I didn't have much money. My husband refused me nothing. He gave me what I needed for the housekeeping and never asked me to account for my spending. But I couldn't misappropriate large sums without talking to him about it.

'So Philippe would cunningly go and speak to René in secret . . . He would tell him the same story, or another, and urge him not to discuss it with me.'

'On what terms did your brother leave Rue du Saint-Gothard?'

'We discovered that he had been behaving dishonestly . . . It was all the more serious since he had gone to see important customers and asked them for money on behalf of my husband.'

'And your husband finally got angry with him?'

'He had a long talk with him. Instead of giving Philippe a sum of money to be rid of him, he arranged for him to receive a monthly allowance that was sufficient for him to live on . . . I imagine you can guess the rest?'

'He came back asking for more.'

'And, each time, we forgave him. Each time, he gave the impression that he was really going to start a new life . . . We opened our door to him again . . . Then he disappeared after committing a new offence.

'He lived in Bordeaux . . . He swore he'd got married there, that there was a child, a daughter, but, if it was true, we never saw any evidence other than the photo of a woman who could be anyone. As I was saying, even if it was true, he soon abandoned his wife and daughter to go and live in Brussels.

'There, again according to him, he was in danger of being thrown into prison, and my husband sent him some money.

'I don't know whether you understand . . . It's difficult, without knowing him . . . He always sounded sincere and I think in a way he was . . . He's not a bad person . . .'

'But even so, he killed your husband.'

'Until I have proof and he admits it, I refuse to believe it . . . And I'll always have a slight doubt . . . I'll always wonder whether it's not my fault . . .'

'How long was it since he'd been to Rue Notre-Dame-des-Champs?'

'You mean our apartment?'

'I don't understand the difference.'

'Because he hasn't set foot in our home for at least seven years . . . It was after Brussels and before Marseille, when Véronique wasn't yet married . . . Until then he had always dressed smartly – he was very elegant, well groomed – he came back looking almost like a tramp and it was obvious that he'd gone hungry . . .

'He'd never been so humble, so repentant. We let him stay with us for a few days and, since he claimed to have a job waiting for him in Gabon, once again my husband helped him get back on his feet.

'We heard nothing from him for nearly two years . . . Then, one morning when I was on my way out to the shops, I found him waiting for me outside, on the corner of the street.

'I won't tell you his latest story . . . I gave him a little money.

'The same thing has happened several times in the past few years . . . He swore he hadn't contacted René, that he'd never ask him for anything ever again.'

'And the same day he arranged to see him?'

'Yes. As I told you, he continued to hedge his bets. I've had evidence since yesterday.'

'How?'

'I had a feeling . . . I knew you would probably find out about Philippe's existence and that you would ask me detailed questions.'

'You hoped that it would be as late as possible to give him time to get out of the country?'

'Wouldn't you have done the same thing? . . . Do you not think that your wife, for instance, would have done the same?'

'He killed your husband.'

'Supposing that is proven, he's still my brother, and putting him in prison for the rest of his life won't bring René back . . . I know Philippe . . . But if one day I have to tell a jury what I've just told you, they won't believe me . . . He's a poor soul, not a criminal.'

What was the point of arguing with her? And it was true, in a way, that Philippe de Lancieux was an unlucky man.

'I was telling you that I was going through my husband's papers, in particular his cheque stubs, of which there are two drawerfuls, carefully filed, because he was meticulous. And that was how I found out that each time Philippe had come to see me, he also went to see my husband, at Rue du Saint-Gothard initially, and then, later, I don't know where . . . He probably waited for him in the street, as he did me.'

'Your husband never mentioned it to you?'

'He didn't want to upset me. And meanwhile I . . . If we'd been more open with one another, perhaps nothing would have happened . . . I've thought about it a lot . . . On Wednesday, just before midday, before René got back, I received a telephone call and I immediately recognized Philippe's voice.'

Had he been calling from the Brasserie Franco-Italienne, where he'd just met Josselin? It was likely. That could be verified. The woman at the till might remember giving him a token.

'He told me he absolutely had to see me, that it was a matter of life and death and that afterwards we would never hear from him again . . . He told me to meet him at the café, as you know. I went there on my way to the hairdresser's.'

'One moment. Did you tell your brother that you were going to the hairdresser's?'

'Yes . . . I wanted to explain to him why I was in such a hurry.'

'And did you mention the theatre?'

'Wait . . . I'm almost certain . . . I must have said:

'"I have to get my hair done because I'm going to the theatre with Véronique this evening."

'He seemed even more on edge than on the other occasions . . . He told me he'd done something very stupid, without saying what, but he implied that he could be arrested . . . He needed a large sum of money to get to

South America . . . I had in my bag all the money I'd been able to get hold of and I gave it to him.'

'I don't understand why he would have come to our apartment that evening to kill my husband . . .'

'Did he know the revolver was in the drawer?'

'It's been there for at least fifteen years, probably longer, and, at that time, Philippe sometimes stayed with us, as I told you.'

'He also knew, of course, where the key was kept in the kitchen.'

'He didn't take any money . . . Even though there was some in my husband's wallet, he didn't touch it. There was also money in the writing desk and jewellery in my bedroom.'

'Did your husband write out a cheque to Philippe on the day he died?'

'No.'

There was a silence during which they looked at one another.

'I think,' sighed Maigret, 'that that's the explanation.'

'You think my husband said no?'

'It's likely . . .'

Or perhaps he merely gave his brother-in-law a few banknotes that he had in his pocket?

'Did your husband have his cheque book on him?'

If he hadn't, he could have arranged to meet Philippe in the evening.

'He always kept it in his pocket.'

In that case, it was Lancieux who, having failed in the morning, had come back to try again. Had he already decided to kill? Did he hope that once his sister was in charge of the fortune, he would get more out of her?

Maigret did not try to go that far. He had shed as much light on the characters involved as was possible, and the rest would be up to the courts, one day.

'You don't know how long he had been in Paris?'

'I swear I don't have the slightest idea. My only hope, I confess, is that he managed to get out of the country and that we will hear no more of him.'

'What if he were to ask you for money again one day? . . . If you received a telegram, for example from Brussels, Switzerland or elsewhere, asking you to send him a money order?'

'I don't think . . .'

She didn't finish her sentence. For the first time, she avoided Maigret's gaze and stammered:

'You don't believe that either.'

This time there was a long silence and Maigret fiddled with one of his pipes and decided to fill it and light it, which he had refrained from doing during the interview.

There was nothing left to say, and they felt it. Madame Josselin opened her bag again to put away her handkerchief and snapped it shut. That was like a signal. After hesitating one last time, she rose to her feet, holding herself less stiffly than when she had arrived.

'You no longer need me?'

'Not for the time being.'

'I presume you're going to have the police look for him?'

He merely lowered his eyelids. Then, walking over to the door, he said:

'I don't even have a photograph of him.'

'I know you won't believe me, but I don't have one either, other than photos from before the war, when he was just a youth.'

Maigret half-opened the door. They stood there a little awkwardly as if they didn't know how to part company.

'Are you going to question my daughter?'

'That will no longer be necessary.'

'She's perhaps the one who has suffered the most these last few days . . . My son-in-law too, I imagine . . . They didn't have the same reasons to keep quiet . . . They did it for me.'

'I don't hold it against them.'

He extended a hesitant hand and she placed her hand in it, having put her glove back on.

'I won't say good luck,' she stammered.

And, without turning around, she made her way to the waiting room, where an anxious Véronique jumped to her feet.

8.

Winter was over. Ten times, twenty times, the lights stayed on late into the evening, and even into the night, which meant each time that a man or a woman was sitting in the chair that Madame Josselin had occupied, facing Maigret's desk.

A description of Philippe de Lancieux had been circulated to every police station and they were looking for him in the railway stations and at the border posts and the airports. Interpol had opened a file on him which had been sent to foreign police forces.

It wasn't until the end of March, however, when the chimney pots took on their pink hue against the pale blue sky and the trees were beginning to blossom, that Maigret, arriving at his office one morning, without an overcoat for the first time that year, heard the name of Madame Josselin's brother again.

She still lived in the apartment in Rue Notre-Dame-des-Champs with a housekeeper, and went every afternoon to see her grandchildren at Boulevard Brune and take them for a walk in the Parc Montsouris.

Philippe de Lancieux had just been found dead, with several stab wounds, at around three o'clock in the morning, near a bar in Avenue des Ternes.

The newspapers wrote: 'Gangland killing'.

It was more or less true, as always. While Lancieux had never belonged to the crime world, for the past few months he had been living with a prostitute called Angèle.

He continued to make up stories and Angèle was convinced that if he was in hiding at her place, going out only at night, it was because he had escaped from Fontevrault prison, where he had been serving a twenty-year sentence.

Had others realized that he was only a small-time operator? Had they punished him for taking the young woman from her regular protector?

A half-hearted investigation was opened, as is usual in such cases. Maigret had to go to Rue Notre-Dame-des-Champs one more time; again, he saw the concierge, whose baby was burbling away in a highchair. He walked up to the third floor and pressed the bell.

Madame Manu still worked in the apartment for a few hours every day, even though Madame Josselin now had a live-in housekeeper, and it was she who opened the door, taking the chain off this time.

'It's you!' she said, frowning, as if he could only be the bearer of bad news.

Was it such bad news?

Nothing had changed in the drawing room, except that a blue scarf lay on René Josselin's armchair.

'I'll inform Madame.'

'Please.'

Even so, he felt the need to mop his brow as he glanced at himself in the mirror.

OTHER TITLES IN THE SERIES

And more to follow